4
SUGAR CREEK GANG
The LOST CAMPERS

Paul Hutchens

MOODY PUBLISHERS
CHICAGO

All Scripture quotations are taken from the *New American
Standard Bible*, © 1960, 1962, 1963, 1968, 1971, 1972,
1973, 1975, 1977, and 1994 by The Lockman Foundation,
La Habra, Calif. Used by permission.

Cover Design: Ragont Design
Cover Illustration: Don Stewart

Original Title: *Sugar Creek Gang Goes Camping*

ISBN-13: 978-0-8024-7008-9
Printed by Bethany Press in Bloomington, MN – 07/2017

We hope you enjoy this book from Moody Publishers.
Our goal is to provide high-quality, thought-provoking
books and products that connect truth to your real needs
and challenges. For more information on other books
and products written and produced from a biblical per-
spective, go to www.moodypublishers.com or write to:

Moody Publishers
820 N. LaSalle Boulevard
Chicago, IL 60610

19 20 18

Printed in the United States of America

PREFACE

Hi—from a member of the Sugar Creek Gang!

It's just that I don't know which one I am. When I was good, I was Little Jim. When I did bad things—well, sometimes I was Bill Collins or even mischievous Poetry.

You see, I am the daughter of Paul Hutchens, and I spent many an hour listening to him read his manuscript as far as he had written it that particular day. I went along to the north woods of Minnesota, to Colorado, and to the various other places he would go to find something different for the Gang to do.

Now the years have passed—more than fifty, actually. My father is in heaven, but the Gang goes on. All thirty-six books are still in print and now are being updated for today's readers with input from my five children, who also span the decades from the '50s to the '70s.

The real Sugar Creek is in Indiana, and my father and his six brothers were the original Gang. But the idea of the books and their ministry were and are the Lord's. It is He who keeps the Gang going.

PAULINE HUTCHENS WILSON

The *Sugar Creek Gang* Series:

1

There was a big flood in Sugar Creek that spring. Do you remember the time we went to see Old Man Paddler at his cabin in the hills? I guess there never was a snowstorm like that one either. It snowed and snowed and kept on snowing nearly all winter, and that's the reason there was such a big flood in Sugar Creek when all that snow melted.

But if there hadn't been a flood in which Little Jim and I almost got drowned, then later on in the summer—when the gang was up north on our camping trip—maybe Poetry and Dragonfly and I all three *would* have drowned. Poetry and Dragonfly and Little Jim are the names of some of the boys in our gang. I'll introduce you to them in a minute. So before I can tell you about the tangled-up adventures we had up north, I'll have to give you a chapter or two on the famous Sugar Creek flood.

You see, all that snow melting and running across the fields and down the hills into Sugar Creek made him angry. After he woke up out of his long winter's sleep, he got out of bed (creek bed) and ran wild all over the country. His fierce brown water sighed and hissed and boiled and roared and spread out over the cornfields and the swamp and the bayou like a savage octopus reaching out his long, brown water-fingers. He caught pigs and cows and logs and even barns and whirled them all downstream, turned them over and over, and smashed them against rocks and cliffs.

Well, a boy isn't always to blame for all the trouble he gets into. Certainly Little Jim and I weren't to blame for there being so much snow that winter, and we couldn't help it that it rained so hard and so much in the spring and caused the flood that was actually the worst flood in the history of Sugar Creek.

Although maybe I *shouldn't* have put Little Jim into a big washtub and towed him out through the shallow water to his dad's hog house, which was standing in water about two feet deep. But Little Jim's kitten was up on the top of the hog house, meowing like everything, and it looked like the water might get higher. Maybe the kitten—which was a very cute blue-and-white one with an all-white face and a half-white tail—would be drowned, we thought, so we decided to rescue it before the water crept up any higher. And we might just as well have a lot of fun while we were doing it.

Even a boy knows better than to make a raft and float on it out into a mad creek, and we wouldn't have tried to do such a silly thing, but what we did do turned out to be almost as dangerous. You see, Little Jim's dad's low, flat-roofed hog house was standing in very quiet water that had backed up from the bayou into their barnyard. It didn't look a bit dangerous to do what we decided to do. In fact, it wasn't, when we started to go out to where the kitten was. And it wouldn't have been at all, if the dike way up along Sugar Creek hadn't broken and let loose a wall of water about three feet high. It came rushing upon us and—but that's getting ahead of the story.

Let me introduce the gang first, in case you've never heard about us. There were just six of us up until the time Tom Till joined, and when he joined that made the number seven, which is a perfect number.

First, and best, in our gang was Little Jim, a good-looking kid with shining blue eyes, and a great little Christian. For a while he had about all the religion there was in the Sugar Creek Gang, until the rest of us woke up to the fact that to be a Christian didn't mean that you had to be sad and wear a long face or be a girl. And we found out that Jesus Himself was a boy once, just our size, and He liked boys even better than our parents do.

Then there was Big Jim, our leader, who had a baby-sized mustache that looked like the fuzz that grows on a baby pigeon. He was the best fighter in the county, and he'd licked the stuffings out of Tom Till's big brother, Bob. Did I tell you the Till boys' dad wasn't a Christian?— that being the reason Tom and Bob didn't know anything about the Bible and were as mean as an angry old setting hen when you try to break up her nest.

Big Jim and Little Jim weren't brothers but

were just friends, liking each other maybe better than any of us liked the rest of us. Unless it was the way I liked Poetry, which is the name of the barrel-shaped member of our gang, who knows 101 poems by heart and is always quoting one and who has a mind that is like a detective's. Poetry had a squawky voice like a young rooster learning to crow, and he growled half bass and half soprano when he tried to sing in church.

Then there was Circus, our acrobat, who turned handsprings and somersaults and liked to climb trees better than a healthy boy likes to eat strawberries. Circus's dad had been an alcoholic, you know, but something happened to him, which the pastor of our church called being "born again," and after that he was the grandest man a boy could ever have for a father. Except, of course, my own dad, who must have been the best man in the world or my mom wouldn't have picked him out to marry.

Boy oh boy! You ought to meet my brownish-gray-haired mom and my neat baby sister, Charlotte Ann. Mom isn't exactly pretty like Little Jim's mom, but she's got the nicest face I ever saw. Even when she isn't saying a word to me, I can feel her face saying nice things to me and Dad and Charlotte Ann, kind of like wireless telegraphy or something.

Let me see—where was I? Oh, yes. I was telling you about the gang. Dragonfly's the only one I haven't mentioned. He's the pop-eyed one of the gang. He has eyes that make me think of a walleyed pike and especially of a dragonfly, which has two great big eyes that are almost as large as its head, which of course Dragonfly's aren't. But they're big anyway, and his nose doesn't point straight out the way a boy's nose ought to but turns south right at the end. But after you've played with him a few times and know what a great guy he is, you forget all about him being as homely as a mud fence, and you like him a lot. Well, that's us: Big Jim and Little Jim, and Poetry and Circus, and Dragonfly and red-haired me, Bill Collins. Maybe I ought to tell you that I have a fiery temper that sometimes goes off just like a firecracker and is always getting me into trouble.

And now, here goes the story of the flood that was the worst flood in the history of Sugar Creek. Even Old Man Paddler, the kind, white-whiskered old man who lives up in the hills and was one of the pioneers of the Sugar Creek territory, can't remember any flood that was worse.

That old man knows so many important things, and he can tell some of the most exciting tales of the Sugar Creek of long ago. Maybe someday I'll see if I can coax him into writing about the terrible blizzard of 1880 and of the old trapper whom the Indians got jealous of because he caught so many more beavers than they did. They shot him through the heart with an arrow one morning while he was setting his traps. Old Man Paddler has told us boys that story many times.

Well, after we'd saved the old man's life

that cold, snowy day, which I told you about in my last book, *The Winter Rescue,* and after my dad and Circus's dad and a lot of other men had waded through the storm up into the hills to get us—and after we finally got home safely the next day—it began to snow and snow, and all the roads were blocked, and we had to actually dig a tunnel through the big drift next to our barn before we could get in.

After a while, though, a nice long while in which Charlotte Ann kept on growing and learning to say "Daddy" and to sit up without being propped with a pillow, spring began to come. First, there'd be a nice warm day, then a cold one, then rain and more rain, and a warm day again. Then one day in late March, old Sugar Creek started to wake up from his long winter's nap.

About a week before the actual flood, when the creek was still frozen, our gang was standing on the big bridge that goes across the deepest and widest part, looking down at the dirty, snow-covered, slushy-looking ice. And all of a sudden we heard a deep rumbling roar that started right under the bridge and thundered all the way up the creek toward the spring, sounding like an angry thunderclap with a long noisy tail dragging itself across the sky.

Little Jim cried out as though someone had hurt him. "What *is* that?" He looked as if he was afraid, which he is sometimes.

And Big Jim said, *"That?* That's the ice cracking. It's breaking up, and in a few days maybe it'll all break and crack up into a million pieces and go growling downstream, and when it does, it'll be something to look at! See those big ugly scars on that old elm tree over there? Away up high almost to the first limb? That's where the ice crashed against it last year. See where the paint is knocked off the bridge abutment down there? The ice was clear up there last year."

Crash! Roar-r-r-zzzz! The ice was breaking up all right because it was a warm day and all the snow was melting too.

We stayed there watching Sugar Creek's frozen old face, and I thought about all the nice fish that were down under there. And I was wondering if maybe the radio report was right, that it was going to rain for a week beginning that very night, and what'd happen to the little fishies who got lost from their parents and in the swift current were whirled away downstream to some other part of the country.

Well, the radio was right. It began to rain that night, and it kept right on. The ice melted and broke and began to float downstream. It gathered itself into great chunks of different sizes and shapes and looked like a million giant-sized ice cubes out of somebody's refrigerator, only they acted as though they were alive. The brown water of Sugar Creek pushed them from beneath and squeezed its way out through the cracks between pieces and ran over the top, churning and boiling and grinding and cracking and roaring and sizzling and fussing like an old setting hen.

I tell you, it was a great sight to see and great to listen to, and we had the feeling all the time that something was going to happen.

And something did happen—not that day but soon after that, on a Saturday. I had gone over to Little Jim's house on an errand for Mom, although she and I had just made up an errand so I'd have a good excuse to go over there.

You see, Little Jim's pet bear had had to be sold to the zoo. It was getting too big to be a pet and was sometimes very cross and might get angry someday and hurt somebody. Little Jim's parents had bought a blue-and-white kitten for him so that he wouldn't be so lonesome. As I told you, the kitten's face was all white, and it had a half-white tail, making it about the prettiest kitten I ever saw.

I had on my hip-high rubber boots when I came sloshing into Little Jim's backyard about two o'clock that afternoon, just as he was finishing practicing his piano lesson, which was a hard piece by somebody named Liszt.

The sun was shining down very hot for a spring day. I could hear Sugar Creek sighing about a fourth of a mile down the road, and I wished we could go down there and watch the flood. But our parents wouldn't let us stand on the bridge anymore, because it wasn't safe. Some bridges farther up the creek had actually been washed out.

The water had filled up the old swamp and the bayou that was on Little Jim's dad's farm, backing way up into their barnyard and making their straw stack look like a big brownish-yellow island in a dirty brown lake.

Little Jim finished his piano lesson and came out to where I was.

"Hi, Little Jim," I said, and he said, "Hi, Bill."

He still had a sad expression on his face because he didn't have any baby bear to play with.

"I came over to borrow some baking soda," I said. "How's the new kitten today? Where is he? I want to see him. Boy, it sure is a pretty day. Wish we could go down and watch the flood."

He grinned at all the different things I had said, and he sighed and mumbled, "I'd rather have my bear back."

"You could have a bare back if you tore your shirt on a barbed wire," I said, trying to be funny and not being.

And just then I saw his little blue-and-white cat out in their barnyard on top of the hog house. It was a brand new hog house about four feet high and had a board floor, Little Jim told me. He knew because his dad and he had built it themselves. They hadn't even set it up on its foundation yet.

The kitten looked lonesome. How it got up there we didn't know, unless it had been trying to catch a mouse and the water had crept up on it unawares. Anyway, there it was, and it was meowing like everything and looking like a boy feels when he's lost.

It looked like a rescue job for lifeguards, which all of a sudden Little Jim and I decided we were.

"Let's go out and get him," I said.

There really wasn't any danger, for the water wasn't moving. It had backed up from the bayou and was just standing there making a big dirty lake in their barnyard.

"We ought to have a boat," I said, looking around for something that might be good to ride in.

It was Little Jim's idea, not mine, to get his mom's washtub. It wouldn't be big enough for two of us, but it would hold Little Jim, and I had on boots anyway and could pull him. Then when we got there, we could put the kitten in the tub too, and I could pull them both back to shore, the "shore" being the side of a little hill right close to the barn.

It didn't take us more than a jiffy to get the tub and to get Little Jim squatted down in the middle of it and me on the other end of a long rope, pulling him out to the hog house.

Squash, squash, slop, splash went my big rubber boots, and Little Jim floated along behind me, grinning and holding onto the sides of the tub with both hands and with his teeth shut tight, trying not to act scared.

"Where's your dad?" I asked when we were halfway out to the kitten, which was meowing even worse than before.

"He and Big Jim's daddy are up at the other end of the bayou piling up sacks of sand,"

Little Jim said, "so the water won't break over and flood our cornfield. Because if it does, it'll wash out all the wheat Dad sowed between the rows last fall."

Well, we didn't know very much about floods, except that when we were little we'd heard about one on the Ohio River. But anyway, we were having a lot of fun, so we went on out through the muddy water toward the hog house.

Pretty soon we were there, and Little Jim and I climbed up on top of it and sat there in the sun, pretending we were on an enchanted island and were pirates. Then we were ship-wrecked sailors.

We put the cute little fuzzy kitten in the tub and pushed it out into the water—the tub, I mean—with the kitten in it. Kitty didn't seem to mind that, so we left him there while we told stories we'd read in books and talked about our coming camping trip up north and how much fun we'd have and a lot of things. I tied the end of the rope around my leg so Kitty wouldn't drift away.

And all the time, *time* was passing, and the snow up in the hills was melting, and all the little rivers and branches that ran into Sugar Creek kept on emptying themselves. And all the time, the men were up there at the head of the bayou stacking big sacks of sand on the levee that protected Little Jim's dad's field from the flood.

Then, just as time does when a boy is having a lot of fun, two whole hours went past, and all of a sudden Little Jim said, "Look, Bill! The water's getting higher! It's almost—*look out!*" And then he began to scream, "We're moving! We're—" He turned as white as a piece of typewriter paper, and he grabbed hold of me so tight his nails dug into my arm.

I believed it and didn't believe it both at the same time. I looked down at the water, which was certainly a lot higher than it had been. The back side of the hog house was sliding down deeper. I knew what had happened. That back end was set right at the edge of a little hill, and the water had crept up and washed the dirt away from underneath it. And quick as a flash I knew we were in for it.

I looked toward the river and the bayou, and there was a big log spinning toward us. The dark, swirling, muddy water was carrying cornstalks and tree branches and pieces of wood and all kinds of debris, and the log was headed toward us.

Straight toward us, faster and faster! It looked as if all of Sugar Creek was running over the cornfield below us and that it had picked up all the woodpiles in the country and was carrying them away.

Little Jim held onto me, and I held onto him, and we both held onto the roof of the hog house, knowing that if the hog house slid down the hill a little farther, it'd turn over or slide right out into the current, and we'd be carried away. I tell you I was scared, *so* scared that I was numb all over and couldn't think straight.

Then, with a terrible grinding roar, that big log crashed into the side of our hog house. And that was the only thing that was needed to break it loose and start it moving. In seconds there we were, floating away, twisting around and around but *not* turning over! And we were being carried down toward the big bridge where Sugar Creek was the maddest of all.

"We—we're *g-gone!*" Little Jim said, his teeth chattering. And then that little fellow, because he was a wonderful Christian, said, "It's better for us to d-drown than it would be for Little Tom Till or Big B-Bob, 'cause th-they're not saved."

Imagine that! He knew that if we'd drowned right there we would have gone straight to heaven! And that's a lot more than a lot of the smartest people in the world know.

2

I tell you, it's a funny feeling, riding on the top of a hog house in flood waters. I guess we weren't moving nearly as fast as we thought we were, but we *were* moving around in little circles, doing whatever the water wanted us to.

If we hadn't been so scared, it would have been funny, because coming right along behind us was Little Jim's mom's big washtub with that little white-faced, blue-and-white kitten sitting in it and looking even more scared than we felt.

Well, I'd heard of boys tying tin cans to a cat's tail, but I'd never heard of a washtub with a cat in it being tied to a boy's leg. For some reason it didn't seem very funny at the time, especially when I saw Little Jim's face and thought, *What if we do drown! What if we never see our parents again or any of the gang!*

And all the time we were drifting out across the field, getting nearer and nearer to the main part of Sugar Creek, where he was madder than a nestful of bumblebees. We weren't drifting straight toward the bridge, though, but toward the road, which was up on a high embankment. It looked as if we would bump into the bank first and then follow the current along the edge until it got to the bridge.

And there, unless something stopped us, the fierce brown current would grab us and whirl us under the bridge. We'd come out on the other side, right in the worst part of the creek, and go lickety-sizzle straight toward the big island down below the bridge, where there were some tall trees. Maybe we'd bump into one of them and be stopped and could catch hold of a branch and climb up into a tree.

"Look!" Little Jim cried. "There's somebody running down the road!"

Sure enough there was, and it was Circus, our acrobat. He was running and yelling and waving his arms and trying to get to the place where we were going to hit the bank before we did. I guess a million thoughts started wrestling around in my head.

And then I saw a telephone pole at the foot of the embankment, and I knew what Circus was hollering about. And then there he was out in the water, swimming toward that telephone pole. It was a race between him and us, but he got there first and wrapped his legs around the pole just the way he does around a tree when he's climbing one.

And just that second we went racing past, with the cat in the tub swishing along behind us.

You should have seen Circus's right foot shoot out like an octopus's tentacle grabbing for a man. Quicker'n a flash he'd wrapped it around the rope that was fastened to the tub on one end and to my leg on the other.

Before I knew what was happening, I was jerked loose from the roof of the hog house and from Little Jim and was out in the water.

As long as Circus was holding onto the rope with his foot, I knew that if I could get to the telephone pole we'd be saved. But it all happened so suddenly that I went under. I came up sputtering and trying to swim.

Just as I caught hold of the rope with one hand, I looked back, and there was Little Jim lying on his stomach on the flat roof of the hog house, drifting swiftly toward the bridge and toward the maddest part of old Sugar Creek. I could see his face, still as white as a piece of typewriter paper.

He waved an awkward right arm toward us and yelled in a trembly voice, *"Good-bye!"* Then he turned around and grabbed hold of the roof with both hands and was whirled away.

I tell you, it didn't feel very good to know that I was being rescued and that my best friend might not be. All I could see for a minute, while pulling myself by the rope toward the telephone pole, was Little Jim's sad face. And there kept ringing in my ears the words he'd said a little while before that—"It's better for us to d-drown than it would be for Little Tom Till or Big B-Bob, 'cause they're not saved!"

And I made up my mind right that minute that it was the silliest thing in the world for anybody in the world not to repent of his sins and let Jesus save him, because you could never tell what minute something might go wrong and you'd have to die. It's crazy not to be ready. It's the most ridiculous thing in the world!

Even while I was thinking that, and Circus and I were working our way back to the steep bank that led up to the road—saving the kitten at the same time—I kept wondering if it was too late to help Little Jim. *Maybe,* I thought, *if we could get up to the road and make a dash for the bridge, we could get there in time to reach down and catch Little Jim by the arms and pull him up.* The water was pretty high there, and if he would stand up, we could reach him easily.

Quicker than it takes to tell, we were up the bank. I untied the tow rope, and then, leaving the tub and the cat, we were running *squash, squash, kerslosh* down the road in our wet clothes toward the bridge. I was feeling like a boy does in a dream when some wild animal is after him. He can't run fast enough to get away, and then pretty soon he wakes up and finds out it isn't so. And after he gets over being scared, he is happy again. But I knew that this wasn't any dream, and I'd have given anything in the world, *anything,* to save Little Jim's life.

And it's a good thing Circus's parents were poor. If they hadn't been, Circus would probably have been wearing boots like the rest of the kids in the neighborhood, and he couldn't have run so fast. You should have seen him run! Lickety-sizzle, like a flash of lightning, he went down that road, leaving me far behind, his feet throwing sand and gravel behind him the way a horse's hooves do when it's galloping.

Panting, gasping, half crying, crazy old tears getting into my eyes, I stumbled on after Circus, not having sense enough to take off my boots so I could run faster. Watching him, I couldn't help but think of a football game, with the quarterback carrying the ball through a whole tangled-up mess of players toward the goal.

Except that Circus wasn't carrying a football but something a million times better. He was carrying the grandest heart a guy ever had, a heart that was full of honest-to-goodness love for Little Jim. I'll bet if the angels that the Bible says are looking after boys and girls were watching Circus streaking down the road to save Little Jim's life, they felt proud of him and felt like screaming for him to hurry up. Only I don't suppose angels ever scream.

You know, the Bible says in one place, where it's talking about children, "Their angels in heaven continually see the face of My Father who is in heaven." Jesus said that Himself, and He ought to know, because He was in heaven before He came down to earth to be our Savior. He'd seen maybe a million angels up there.

Just that minute I stumbled over a rock in the road and went sprawling. When I got up and started toward the bridge again, I heard somebody yelling for me to hurry, which I did, not even much feeling the bruised place on my right hand where the skin was all scratched off the knuckles of two fingers from the gravel where I'd fallen.

In a minute I was there, but I couldn't see

anybody, not even Circus. Away out in the swiftest part of the creek, heaving and whirling, was the hog house, *and nobody was on it!*

"Hurry up! Quick, Bill!" I heard Circus yelling from down below somewhere.

And I tell you, I hurried, looking all the time and yet afraid to look below for fear I'd see both Little Jim and Circus down there in the water. As quick as my old waterlogged boots would let me, I was where I'd heard Circus's voice.

And there, with his legs wrapped around one of the steel beams that stretched from one support of the bridge to another, was Circus, hanging head down and with his arms around Little Jim, holding onto him for dear life.

And Little Jim was holding onto Circus and swaying back and forth. His feet were almost touching the water, which was all foam-covered and full of cornstalks and slabs of ice.

And even while I looked, out of the corner of my eye I saw the hog house bump into a tree downstream and whirl around and turn over on its side.

In a tenth of a jiffy I was helping Little Jim climb up Circus's body to the bridge floor, where he was safe. And then I started to help Circus, whose face was very red from hanging down like that, and his legs were trembling as if they couldn't have held on another minute. I braced my feet against the iron girders, and with Little Jim helping a little, but not much because he was weak from being so scared, I gave Circus just enough of a pull to help him up to safety too.

The very minute he knew he was safe, he just flopped onto the floor of the bridge the way an athlete does after he's run in a terrible race, and he gasped and panted and his breast heaved up and down.

But Little Jim was safe, and so was I. And good old Circus was safe too. We were all trembling and weak but very happy.

I thought I heard Circus say something under his breath about "lifted me."

"What'd you say, Circus?" I asked.

And he said, "Nothing," but after a while, when we were on the way back to Little Jim's house, I heard Circus singing. He had a beautiful voice for a boy, and Little Jim's mom had been giving him voice lessons free, and he liked to sing church hymns very much. He even sang in church sometimes, when they wanted him to. And what do you suppose Circus was singing? I wouldn't let him know I noticed, or he might have stopped—a boy nearly always starts to feel bashful when he knows somebody is listening to him. But this is the chorus of the song:

> Love lifted me, love lifted me,
> When nothing else could help,
>   Love lifted me;
> Love lifted me, love lifted me,
> When nothing else could help,
>   Love lifted me.

24

So away we went, I with my high rubber boots going *splash, swish, kerslosh* through the puddles in the road. Circus, even though his shoes were very wet, was dodging all the big ones because his mother had taught him not to walk in mud puddles.

And Little Jim was still dry, because he hadn't even gotten his feet wet. He could hardly wait until we got back to where his kitten was—and it was still there, sitting down beside the washtub, looking lonesome.

You should have seen Little Jim scoop up that little white-faced kitty and hug it. Circus and I carried the washtub between us on the way to Little Jim's house, and pretty soon Little Jim decided to let the kitten ride in it. He walked happily along behind us, looking up at Circus as if he thought he was the most wonderful person in the world for saving his life, which I guess he was.

It didn't make any difference that Circus's parents were poor and that he couldn't afford a haircut as often as the rest of the gang. And sometimes his mother had to patch even the patches on his overalls. Circus was all right on the *inside*, which is more important than being rich and at the same time being mean or stingy or keeping your heart's door jammed tight shut against the most important Person in the whole universe.

Well, that's the most interesting part of the flood story, so I'll get busy now and tell you about our camping trip up north, which we took in a trailer that Old Man Paddler bought for his nephew to live in—and to give us a vacation in.

It was when our parents heard about Little Jim's and my crazy boat ride that afternoon that they decided we couldn't go out in real boats when we were up north unless we wore life preservers. And it's a good thing we did, because—

But I'll tell you about that when I get to it, and about a little Indian boy whose name was Snow-in-the-Face, and the railroad car Poetry and I discovered away out in the deep woods up there, and a lot of other exciting things.

3

When old Sugar Creek calmed down after having lost his temper so terribly, his face was as kind and gentle as a lamb's. He had left some of his water standing in little lakes on nearly all our farms. There were fish in them, which we caught not with pole and line but by wading around in the water with our overalls rolled up. We'd wade about until the water got so muddy and thick like gravy that the fish had to stick their noses up for air. Then all we had to do was to walk over, cup our hands under them one at a time, and pull them out, holding on tight so they wouldn't get away.

Pretty soon it was summer and growing hotter all the time—and getting closer and closer to the fifth of July, which was the date on which we were supposed to leave for northern Minnesota on our camping trip. We spent the Fourth of July without shooting off any firecrackers, because one of the boys in our town had burned his hand badly the year before. That had made all our parents extra cautious, so they wouldn't let us have firecrackers.

But we didn't much care, because nobody else was doing it. There was plenty of excitement at our house on the Fourth to satisfy me anyway, just getting things ready.

All the gang had agreed to meet at the spring at two o'clock to talk things over and maybe have a last swim in Sugar Creek. Old Man Paddler's nephew, Barry Boyland, had come from California with his new house trailer. He'd parked it under a big oak tree close to the spring and had been living there for about a week.

There was something especially nice about Mr. Boyland that we all liked. Barry had been a Scout once—still was one, I guess—and he knew all the things a First Class Scout has to know to be one.

Nearly all the gang had already taken their camping equipment to the trailer, and it was planned that we would leave early the next morning. I still had to take my overnight kit down and pack it in with the rest of my luggage —the overnight kit being a long, rectangular piece of waterproof material with pockets for toothbrush, soap, comb, brush, small mirror, and washcloth. When everything was all in it, you rolled it up into a little package. I hadn't wanted to take the washcloth, but Mom said I had to.

Pretty soon it was noon at our house on the Fourth, and it was a terribly hot day again, making me glad we were going up north to where it would be nice and cool. Mom and Dad and Charlotte Ann and I were sitting around our kitchen table, where we nearly always ate at noon except when we had company. I was finishing my piece of blackberry pie, which Mom had baked especially for me because it was my favorite pie. It was the last piece of Mom's pie I'd get for two whole weeks.

I was all a-tingle inside, thinking about tomorrow, feeling very happy, yet kind of sad too. I looked across the table at Charlotte Ann, my one-year-old baby sister. Because she was sleepy, she was leaning over in her high chair the way a willow tree down along Sugar Creek leans over the water, and her pretty blue eyes were half shut. Her little round head with its tangle of black curls was nodding the way a baby's head does, and I felt strange in my heart, as if I was in a big vise that was being squeezed shut on me. *She's a great little sister,* I thought. *In fact, she's wonderful.*

What makes a boy feel that way toward his sister, anyway?

Then I took another bite of pie, using the best table manners I could think of, so my parents would have something pleasant to remember me by while I was away.

I looked at Mom, who was chewing her pie, and at some new gray hair that was mixed with the brown and which I had never noticed before.

Then I looked at Dad, sitting at the head of the table with his sleeves rolled up. The muscles of his brown arms were moving like big ropes that were alive, and they kept moving all the time and making the brown skin bulge out in different places.

They're great parents, I thought, *and I'll bet they'll miss me while I'm away.*

And all of a sudden I wasn't hungry.

"May I be excused?" I asked as courteously as I could. That week I'd been reading a book on courtesy, which my parents had bought for me and which all boys ought to read, and the book had made me decide that if I ever wanted to be anybody important in the world, I'd have to have good manners, even when I was at home.

"Excused?" Mom said with a question mark on the end of her voice. "Why, you haven't finished your pie, Bill! I baked it especially for you."

I looked down at my plate and could hardly believe my eyes. I actually *had* left some of my pie, which goes to show that even blackberry pie isn't the most important thing in the world to a boy who likes his folks. I finished the pie and excused myself again, reminding Mom to be sure to call me as soon as the dishes were ready to be dried.

I went outdoors and down to the barn to say good-bye to the horses and cows and pigs and chickens. And especially to our old black-and-white mother cat, who we called Mixy and who had a whole nestful of brand-new black and white and brown and yellow kittens, with the different colors all mixed up.

Old Mol and Jim, Dad's favorite plow horses, were standing quietly in a big box stall, facing each other. Jim's nose was pushing up against Mol's neck, right where it was fastened onto her head—the way my parents stand sometimes when they're looking down at Charlotte Ann.

Just as I was stooping down to pet Mixy— and to tell her not to feel bad because I was going away and not to worry—I heard a squawky voice behind me.

"Hi, there, Bill Collins!" It was Poetry, who had come puffing into the barn without my knowing he was there.

I jumped as if I was shot, turned around partway, and said, "Hi, there, yourself! Why don't you tell a guy when you're coming? You almost made me jump out of my shoes!" I looked down at my feet, and I didn't have shoes on.

"Sorry," Poetry said, meaning he wasn't. "What you looking at so sober-faced?" He came over to where I was and stood peering down into the corner at Mixy and her big family of awkward little kittens.

All of them had their eyes still shut because they weren't old enough yet to have them open, which baby kittens aren't until they're two weeks old. All of them were eating their dinner in the way baby kittens do. That is, some of them were. The others were waggling and nosing around and getting in each other's way and stumbling over each other and falling down, which didn't hurt them. They were so little they didn't have far to fall, which is why it doesn't hurt a boy to fall down nearly as much as it does a grown-up person.

Old Mixy was looking happy, and her black-and-white tail was waving a little on the end very cheerfully as if she was trying to say, "You aren't the only one to have a nice family. Look at mine!"

Seeing the kittens reminded Poetry of a poem, which he started to quote:

"Six little pigs in the straw with their mother;
  Bright eyes, curly tails, tumbling on each other;
  Bring them apples from the orchard trees
  And hear those piggies say,
    'Please, please, please.'"

Poetry even sang it, because it was in our music book at school, and his voice was so squawky that Mixy actually meowed for him to shut up or he'd wake up her babies—which were already awake without having their eyes open. Anyway, she meowed, and he stopped singing, maybe because I pulled his hat down over his eyes with a jerk and told him to.

From Mixy's house we went out to the edge of our pasture, which was on the south side of the barn and where there was a high straw stack. We climbed on top of it and slid down several times, but it was too hot to play in the sun, so we went back toward the swing in our big walnut tree to get cooled off, and all the time I was half waiting for Mom to call me to help with the dishes, which she didn't.

I had planned on going up into our haymow to sit on the hay and feel sad a while because I was going to be leaving home, but Poetry's coming changed my mood. We decided we would go down to the spring to see the trailer and to meet the gang. Poetry had brought some more of his equipment to take down there any-way—his camera and a new flashlight.

Each one of us boys was taking along a first aid kit, which had in it a lot of different things and which every family ought to have in their medicine cabinet in case anybody gets hurt a little. Ours had waterproof adhesive tape, gauze bandage, cotton, Band-Aids, Mercurochrome, a pair of scissors, and different things like that.

Poetry looked at his watch. "I think the gang'll be there early, so we'd better hurry."

"Just as soon as I get the dishes dried," I said, wishing I didn't have to help do them but not saying so. A gentleman doesn't say every unpleasant thing he thinks, the courtesy book says.

When I got back into the house, Mom and Dad had the dishes nearly all done.

"Why didn't you call me?" I asked, feeling guilty.

"Surprise," Dad said. His big, blackish-red eyebrows were up, and he looked at me as though he liked me a lot.

"Oh, there's Poetry!" Mom said, looking over my shoulder at Leslie Thompson, who was filling most of the doorway behind me. "Want a piece of blackberry pie?" she asked him. "We had too much, and with Bill gone there won't be anybody to eat it."

My parents were like that to all my friends, which is why all the boys in the county liked my parents.

Poetry ate his pie, and then he and I went down through the woods to the spring.

Just as we got to the top of the little hill that leads past the old beech tree to the spring, where the trailer was parked, Barry Boyland started up his big black car and began to drive away. But seeing us, he stopped and waited till we got there.

He was wearing a hat with a Scout insignia embroidered on it and a khaki shirt that was open at the neck and had short sleeves, which let his big brown muscles show like my dad's—and they were almost as big. His face was so tanned it was almost black, and he had a little scar on his cheek where he'd been shot by the police that time I told you about in my story *The Swamp Robber*, when the police thought he was a bank robber.

Barry Boyland had blue eyes that were as blue as a Fourth of July sky. His hair was as black as a piece of coal, and there was one all-gold tooth right in front, which made him look important.

"Here you are, Bill," he said, handing me the key to the trailer. "I have to run into town for half an hour or so. You boys can pack your luggage in the compartment behind the folding bed. I'll stop at your house on the way back and pick up your tent," he said to Poetry.

Holding the key in my hand, I felt important myself to be trusted like that.

None of the rest of the gang were there yet, so Poetry and I decided to go inside and wait, and he could pack his overnight kit and blanket, which each one of us boys had to take with us.

Just as I was inserting the key in the lock, I heard a sound down at the spring. Looking around quick, I saw a red head peeping from behind the big linden tree—or bee tree, as my dad called it, which in June was covered all over with small, sweet-smelling, creamy-yellow flowers, which bees like better than bears like blackberries. The other name for the tree is white basswood.

Well, I knew that head of red hair belonged to Little Tom Till, whose nose I'd smashed once in a fight, and whose big brother Bob was so mean, and who4se father wasn't a Christian, and who had never been to church in his life until I got him started, and who was a great little guy even if he and I both did have red hair.

I finished unlocking the door, pulled it open, and then without knowing I was going to, I called, "Hey, Tom! Want to see what it looks like inside?" All of a sudden I'd remembered a promise I made to myself one day last winter—that someday, if I could, I was going to do something very important for Little Tom Till.

He came out from behind the tree kind of bashful-like, because he didn't belong to the gang, but pretty soon we were inside the trailer, and I was showing him different things. There were a kitchen and dining room and sitting room and bathroom and bedroom and storeroom all in one big long room.

"See here?" I said to Tom, whose blue eyes were open wide with looking. I lifted up a linoleum-topped trapdoor on one end of a worktable and hooked it so it would stay up, and there underneath was a two-burner gas stove, which was connected to a big steel bottle of compressed gas under one of the seats in the dinette, and which you couldn't see without lifting up the seat.

At the other end of the worktable was a sink and a water faucet—only you didn't turn the water on like a faucet in a house but lifted it up and down, and it pumped the water out of a tank under the long seat on the other side of the eating table.

"Want a drink?" I asked Tom and gave him one out of the faucet.

"Where do you sleep?" he asked, looking around and not seeing any beds.

"Right here," Poetry said, flopping down on a neat, blue davenport.

"Seven people sleep *there?*" Tom asked with doubt in his voice.

We laughed.

"No, just two. See?" Poetry jumped up, gave the davenport a quick movement, which made it turn a somersault, and there, as pretty as you please, was a bed wide enough for two or even three boys. All you had to do was to put blankets and pillows and sheets on it, and it'd be ready.

"And some of us'll sleep here," I said, pointing to the dinette. "This table comes out and

36

goes underneath, and these cushions lie across it, making a nice bed for two. And the rest of the gang will sleep outside in tents, which we'll pitch close by when we get up there. We're going to park right beside a big lake where we can go in swimming every morning and every night or anytime we want to. And when we're hungry we'll throw in a line and hook and catch all the fish we want to. There are so many fish up there that they get all tangled up in your lines—"

Poetry interrupted me to say, "And sometimes we use redheaded boys for bait, the fish are so big."

All of a sudden Little Tom Till began to look very sad.

I went on showing him the different conveniences: the refrigerator, the dish cupboards, the heating stove—which was in a little cupboard about the size of a small coat closet—a big two-door clothes closet, and a lot of storage space at the end. There were sockets for electric light bulbs, and a place to attach a radio, with a built-in aerial, and you could get the electricity from the car for the lights, if you wanted to.

All the time Little Tom looked sadder and sadder. Pretty soon, when I looked around, he was gone, out the door and down past the spring, running toward home. I saw him raise his fist up to his eyes and dab at something, which I guessed were tears, and I knew that Tom wanted to go camping with us worse than he wanted to do anything else in the world.

"Here!" I said to Poetry, "hold the key till I get back."

Like a flash I was off down the path after Little Tom Till, calling him to stop, which he wouldn't do. He turned the corner quick, darted down a steep hill, and went underneath the bridge, where he stopped in the shade, panting for breath. When I got down to where he was, he was hanging by his legs from one of the girders under the bridge, pretending to be doing acrobatic stunts.

I liked Tom better and better all the time. As soon as I could, I told him about a promise I'd made myself last winter, and that was that I was going to try to get him to join the Sugar Creek Gang. And then I told him a story Old Man Paddler had told us out of the Bible.

All of a sudden he spoke up and said, "I won't go to Sunday school while you're gone. Do they have any Sunday schools up north?"

"Sure," I said, "and Indians go to them. Did you ever see an Indian?"

Just then I heard his dad calling him, and he got a scared look on his face, turned pale, and started to climb back up from under the bridge. I was scared too, because I couldn't think of old hook-nosed John Till without remembering how mean he was.

"Good-bye," Tom called down to me, and soon I heard his bare feet running lickety-sizzle across the bridge toward home, where he'd probably get a licking for something he hadn't done. His daddy was that kind of a daddy, always giving Tom a licking before he found out for sure whether he needed it. He was not like my dad at all, who always was careful to decide whether I needed to be punished or not.

And then Poetry was down there beside me, and he had a big whiskey bottle in his hand, which he held up for me to see. "Look!" he said. "I found it in Sugar Creek back there by the spring. There's writing inside it!"

The bottle was corked up tight, but, sure enough, there was some paper in it with writing on it, looking like a boy's handwriting. And it was what we found in the bottle that made us decide something very important.

Poetry pulled the cork out, and what do you suppose? There was a letter in it written by Little Tom Till. It said:

> Whoever finds this, please read the little printed tract which tells all about how to be saved and go to heaven, and write to me and tell me if you let Jesus come into your heart.

Tom had signed his name to the letter and put his address right below it.

The tract was one of those leaflets our Sunday school teacher had given us the Sunday before, telling us to pass them out to people. I certainly felt ashamed—I'd left mine in my room all week and forgotten them because I was thinking all the time about our camping trip.

Poetry folded the letter carefully, wrapped the tract around it, pushed it back into the bottle, put the cork in good and tight, and with a very sober face threw it back into the creek. Then he turned to me and said, "I think Tom Till ought to be invited to go with us on our camping trip."

"So do I," I said.

We ran back toward the trailer to wait for Barry and the rest of the gang so we could talk it over with them.

4

Hot! Hot! Hot!
Whew!

That's the way we all felt that Fourth of July. Then came the fifth, just as hot or hotter, but we felt fine and very cheerful because we'd soon be on our way up north.

By nine o'clock we were packed and ready —and had actually started—and all of us felt like yelling, "Hurrah!" when Barry Boyland's big black car with the beautiful silver-topped house trailer on behind glided down the road, across Sugar Creek bridge, and headed north toward the place where we were to camp for two whole weeks.

"Be a man!" my dad said to me while I was still in the house just before leaving. He gave me a half hug, the way he always does when he likes me.

Then Mom gave me a whole hug and said, "Don't forget you're a Christian, Billy-boy!"

Then Dad came over, and we had a big three-cornered hug, which we were always having anyway, especially when I was smaller. While Mom and Dad were hugging me and each other at the same time, I reached down and laid my hand on the top of Charlotte Ann's head, making it a rectangular hug instead of a triangular one. Her little head was round and as soft as a rose petal.

"Do you have your New Testament?" Mom asked.

"Yep," I said indifferently, and that was the last thing I said. But that little "yep" was a promise to read my Bible every day and to act like a Christian.

There were eight of us instead of seven because Little Tom Till got to go too, so there wasn't room enough for us all to ride in the car. Three of us had to ride in the trailer, which was a lot of fun. We took turns, a different group of three every fifty miles, so that we all got a chance to ride in it.

To ride in the trailer was sort of like riding in a train. Barry made us promise to sit still. It was dangerous not to, and if we got to cutting up, it might make the trailer sway and cause an accident.

It was great watching the telephone poles and trees go whizzing past and imagining all the fun that was ahead of us.

Barry drove hard all day, and the road wound round and round, with lakes or forest on either side, nearly all afternoon of that first day. And still we weren't there. At six o'clock we stopped at a lakeside camp and pitched Poetry's tent and another one that we'd brought along.

After supper, which was hot dogs and buns and fruit—the hot dogs being roasted over a campfire—we all played table tennis in a garage close by. Then, when our suppers had settled, we took a swim in the lake, which was only about a hundred feet from camp.

Wow! Talk about cold water! We'd been used to swimming in Sugar Creek, whose water in the summertime was almost hot, but the water of this lake was like ice water at first—until we were used to it. Then it was great.

The sun was still up, although pretty soon it'd go down. The tall trees were making long shadows on the clear blue water, and the little clouds in the east were purple and cream-colored like my mom's irises back home. Some of the clouds looked like the inch-high creamy foam on the top of our milk pail when Dad's finished milking and is carrying the milk toward the house—with old Mixy the cat following along behind or running on ahead or rubbing against his legs and meowing for him to give her her supper.

And then it was dark. We all put on our sweaters or coats, whichever we'd brought along. Barry stirred up the campfire so that the sparks shot up high and the big yellow flames leaped—like Circus's dad's dogs jumping up and down around a tree when there's a coon up there somewhere.

I guess I never will forget that first night. Each one of us told a story—or rather, part of the same story—which Poetry said was a "hash" story because it had so many different things in it and was all mixed up. Big Jim started it, and then when he got to an interesting place he stopped, and Poetry went on from there. Each of us made up his own part as he told it. By the time the story was finished, it was almost time for us to go to bed.

Then Barry Boyland reached over to the campfire with his long stick and stirred up the sparks again, which looked like stars shooting up. We were all around the fire, half lying down and half sitting up, waiting for Barry to give us his special campfire talk, which we were to have every night, that being one of the reasons our parents wanted us to go on our camping trip.

While Barry was talking, I looked across the fire to where Little Tom Till was sitting. His red hair was combed, and his big blue eyes were looking at Barry's brown face, and maybe at the scar on his cheek, and I could tell that he thought Barry was greater even than Abraham Lincoln.

I wished all the boys in the world could have heard what Barry said. It was the story of the prodigal son in the Bible, whose father gave him a lot of money and things. And instead of being sensible and saving his money, the boy took everything and started on a long trip. While he was in a far country, he got into trouble and lived a sinful life, spending all his money—just wasting it—and thinking about himself and being selfish. And all the time his dad was heavyhearted back home because his boy had run away.

Then one day the boy got a job feeding hogs. He got sadder and sadder and hungrier and hungrier and lonesomer and lonesomer.

He was so hungry that he could actually have eaten some of the big long pods of the carob tree, which grew in that country and which were good hog food but not very good for boys. Although Barry said that in time of famine even the people over there in that country used to eat them, making a kind of syrup out of the pulp.

"Boys," Barry said, "the heavenly Father has given each of you a wonderful body, strong and healthy, and a good mind. I hope not one of you will ever waste it by not taking care of it. That you'll never have any habits that'll waste your health or make your mind dirty, but you will be clean and strong. Keep your thoughts pure like . . . like . . ."

Barry stopped talking for almost a minute, it seemed, before he finished that sentence. He pushed his stick into the fire once more, sending up a shower of sparks that looked like big raindrops going up instead of down. Then he started the sentence all over again. "Keep your thoughts pure like *Jesus,* who was God's only begotten Son. The Father in heaven never had to be ashamed of Him."

Things were quiet around the campfire after that until Poetry's squawky voice started to sing a new chorus that Sylvia's dad had taught us. Sylvia's dad, you know, is our new minister back home, who likes kids. Sylvia is a girl in the eighth grade, and Big Jim is always especially polite to her.

The chorus went like this: "It's a grand

thing to be a Christian. It's a grand thing, I know . . ." And pretty soon we were all singing it together, none of us caring that Poetry's voice squawked or that Tom Till couldn't carry a tune very well. You could hear Circus's bell-like voice above all of ours, singing a kind of tenor.

Well, it was time to go to bed, because tomorrow would be there in a jiffy after we got to sleep, and we'd be off again, going still farther north.

Barry and Little Jim and I slept in one tent. Poetry and Dragonfly were in Poetry's tent, and Circus and Big Jim and Little Tom Till were in the trailer.

I went to sleep right away in my sleeping bag —and right away, it seemed, I was wide awake. The luminous dial on my watch, which my parents had given me, said it was two o'clock in the morning. What makes a boy sleep so *fast* anyway? I'd actually slept five whole hours in about half a minute!

For some reason I was wide awake, listening to Barry Boyland's heavy breathing.

Maybe it was Little Jim's wiggling around on his cot right next to me that woke me up. Just that minute he mumbled something in his sleep, and he seemed to be trying to wake up and couldn't. I leaned over and heard him say, "The flood—the water—it's better for us to d-drown than for Tom Till—my kitty—here, kitty, don't be afraid!"

Then he whimpered and twisted in his bed

as if somebody was chasing him and he couldn't run very fast. So I reached up with my kind of rough hand and wriggled it around until I found his little soft one, and all of a sudden he took a great big breath and sighed and was fast asleep with his hand in mine.

And do you know what I thought? It's kind of a secret, and having Little Jim for a friend helps make me think things like this, but I guess it belongs in this story. Anyway, I thought that if I was a prodigal son and had run away from home and wasted my life for a while, and then was terribly sorry and went back home to my parents or to . . . to *God* . . . if He'd just sort of reach out His great big kind hand and put it on mine, I'd know He had forgiven me. And I'll bet, if I was tired, I'd go right to sleep without worrying.

I left my hand on Little Jim's a long time so I wouldn't wake him up when I took it away.

Outside, the waves of the lake were washing up against the shore, washing and washing. And when I pushed my head out through the tent flap, the sky was as clear as the blue on our American flag, and the stars were just as bright, only they twinkled as if they were alive, and for a minute I was lonesome for my parents.

The sky with all the bright stars in it made me think of a big saltshaker that was shaking down little grains of light instead of salt. Or maybe sand, and the sand was getting mixed up with my eyes, making me shut them, and the waves washing on the shore turned into

Barry Boyland's heavy breathing, and then mine . . .

The next thing I knew it was morning, the tent flap was open, Little Jim and Barry were gone, and Poetry was standing over me, dropping little drops of water on my face to make me wake up.

Outside the tent the rest of the gang were hollering and running around, pulling down the other tent, and getting ready to start on the last leg of the trip.

Poetry threw open the tent flap very wide, let the sun in on my eyes, and said:

"A birdie with a yellow bill
  Hopped upon a window sill,
  Cocked his pretty eye and said,
  'Ain't you 'shamed, you sleepyhead!'"

Which I wasn't, but I zipped down my sleeping bag zipper, rolled out, and started off the day with a flying tackle on Poetry's stovepipe-shaped legs.

5

I don't know where I got the idea that the Indians up north would be wearing war bonnets on their heads or have long black hair with all colors of feathers stuck in them. Most of the Indians we saw dressed just like other Americans. The boys and girls and men and women went around the streets with faces that were brown instead of red—otherwise, they looked just like everybody else.

We came driving into the town of Pass Lake, Minnesota, about two o'clock in the afternoon. Barry went into the post office to see if he had any mail and to tell the postmaster to send all our mail out to a place called "The Pines," which was the name of the place where we were going to make camp. The mailman didn't bring mail out there in a car but came put-putting around the lake in a motorboat.

Well, Pass Lake was a lake as well as a town, and that was the name of the lake we camped beside. "The Pines" was the name of the summer resort close by.

We parked our trailer on a lot that was like a park with a neat little cabin on it. It belonged to a man who lived in Chicago, a big round man who looked like Santa Claus except for his not having any whiskers, and he was always laughing and liked boys. We named him Santa Claus right away and called him that all the time we were camped on his lot. And Mrs. Santa Claus! She was a grand little person who looked like Little Jim's mom and had a very special giggle when she laughed.

Santa Claus showed us where to park and helped us pitch the tents. Then he went back to work cutting down small trees on the back of his lot. He'd come up there especially because his doctor in Chicago had wanted him to get more exercise in the open air and see if he could lose ten or twenty pounds of weight that he didn't need.

"See there," I said to Poetry when he and I were driving in tent stakes for his tent, "if you don't get more exercise and stop eating so much pie, you'll have to chop wood to get thin when you grow up."

Poetry grunted, whacked the tent stake hard with the back of his hatchet, and said, "I'd rather be fat and cheerful like Santa Claus than thin and grumpy."

You could tell right away that Mrs. Santa Claus, whose first name was Georgia, liked boys too. Just that minute she came around to where we were and said, *"Psst!* If you boys would like a piece of pie—"

"Of course," Poetry said politely. He wiped his forehead and licked his chops the way a pup does when it sees a piece of steak being held up.

Well, that was the beginning. Different things happened that afternoon, and then we went

swimming in water that was even ⌐
the water in the other lake had been.

That night Santa Claus gave the ca⌐
talk and taught us a new chorus. And the ⌐
day, Poetry and I had a strange adventure.

It happened like this. In the afternoon, Big
Jim and Tom and Barry Boyland took Santa
Claus's big white boat with its outboard motor
and went fishing for walleyed pike, leaving
Poetry, Dragonfly, Circus, Little Jim, and me to
guard the camp and to fish off the dock if we
wanted to.

We didn't want to do that. We'd wanted to
go fishing in the boat and couldn't—three was
enough to go fishing in one boat when you're
trolling, which is a way to fish that I'll tell you
about in another chapter. The five of us who
stayed behind went in swimming and got cooled
off. Then we lay around on blankets in Poetry's
tent.

We even slept, until Santa Claus came over
after having taken *his* afternoon nap, which the
doctor had said he ought to have every day. I
could see right away that Santa Claus was beginning to like Circus very much, there not being any children in his family. Someday they
might adopt a boy from some orphans' home
or somewhere, they said.

Anyway, he asked Circus and Dragonfly and
Little Jim to drive to town with him in his car to
get some minnows, so the rest of us could go
fishing when the boat came back, which would
be along about five o'clock.

etry and me alone at camp. The
was two or three blocks distant
ta Claus's cabin was between us
the other side was forest. And
there somewhere was an Indi-
where, I thought, Indians lived
the way Indians do in the stories we'd read
about in books.

Barry hadn't told us we couldn't take a walk
if we wanted to, and we certainly wanted to, especially since Poetry had his camera along, and
I had my binoculars, and we needed a chance
to use them.

So pretty soon, when Mrs. Santa Claus strolled
over and saw how sad we felt and how much we
wanted to take a walk and do a little exploring,
she laughed with her very special giggle bub-
bling right up out of her throat and said, "I
think this would be the very nicest place to
read my book, so if you boys want to scout
around a little, I'll watch camp for you."

It was as easy as that. So, camera and binoculars in hand and a little homemade map of
the territory with us, we started out.

We followed the shore for a while and every
now and then took a look out into the lake and
far across to where they were trolling for walleyed pike. When we'd gone about what we
thought was a mile, we looked at the map and
then started off straight north toward where
there was supposed to be an Indian reservation
—which means a tract of land reserved for the
Indians to live on.

We walked and walked through dense forest—birch and ash and cottonwood and balsam and spruce. We were studying trees that summer and making a scrapbook of the leaves of different kinds. So whenever we found a new kind, we wrote down its name in a little notebook and picked a leaf, which we put in our hats to take back to camp. Our parents would be glad to know we were interested in things like that.

All of a sudden, Poetry stopped and said, "What time is it?"

I looked at my little black-faced watch with its white numbers, and it was almost four o'clock already.

"We ought to be close to the Indian reservation by now," he said, taking out the homemade map. "Let me see. This is south, and this is north. We've been walking straight north for a half hour."

"Have we?" I said. "I thought we turned east back there at the big pine tree."

"East?" Poetry said. "That's where we turned *north!*"

"We did not," I said, and just that minute we heard a sound that sounded like somebody screaming with a quavering voice. We'd heard that a few times before since we'd come up north, and Barry'd told us it was a loon, a diving bird that has very short tail feathers and sounds like a screech owl with a ghost's voice.

Well, if that was a loon, then we knew we were close to a lake. We listened. The sound had come from behind us. But the lake couldn't be *behind* us, because we'd just turned around.

Poetry and I looked at each other, puzzled.

It was about time to start back to camp, and we hadn't found any Indian reservation. Then we heard the cry of the loon again, and this time it was in just the opposite direction, which it couldn't have been if the bird had been where it was before! I stood there all mixed up in my mind.

Poetry and I looked straight at each other again.

Then we took out the map and looked at it and laughed at ourselves, because the map showed there was a wagon trail to the north of us and the lake to the south. If we'd go either way, and walk far enough, we'd find either the lake or the wagon trail, and after that all we'd have to do would be to go the right direction, and we'd come out at the camp.

But which was the right direction?

Neither one of us knew, and Poetry didn't have his compass because he'd lost it that snowy day last winter when we'd gone up to see Old Man Paddler—but that's in another story, which you've probably already read.

"If we knew which way was north," I said, "we'd walk to the wagon road. That ought to be closer than trying to find the lake."

"If the road is north, then the lake is south," Poetry said, with his eyebrows down, looking at the map. "Wish that loon'd holler again."

But the loon didn't, and we couldn't tell

from the sun. The sun *looked* as if it was in the north, which it couldn't have been.

I'd never been actually lost in my life, but I began to feel like it, and it's a crazy feeling. Any direction you happen to look is either north or south or east or west *if you think it is*, which it isn't. That's how you feel when you're lost.

Well, we threw ourselves down on the grass in the sunshine, which came down through an opening in the trees overhead.

Poetry had a pucker on his forehead, which meant he was thinking or maybe just trying to. Suddenly he straightened up.

"Give me your watch," he said, and I said, "What for?"

He grinned. "I want to make a compass out of it. I just remembered something I read once." He took my watch and laid it down flat on its back in the sun and looked at it, all the time with that pucker on his forehead.

"Let me see," he said, "one half of what makes what?"

It sounded like some crazy arithmetic problem, and I was never very good in arithmetic. Poetry was the best in his class in school.

All of a sudden he let out a yell. "I've got it! I've got it!" He looked like he'd got *something*. "Quick," he said. "Give me a stick about the size of a match. I'll have the directions straight for you in one minute."

After I saw what Poetry did, I made up my mind that I was going to study arithmetic harder.

With the watch face up, he stood the little

stick straight up at the outside edge of the hour hand. Then he turned the watch around until the stick's shadow fell all along the length of the hour hand, which was, of course, pointing straight toward the sun.

"See there!" Poetry exclaimed cheerfully. "Straight south is just halfway between the hour hand and number twelve on the watch!"

It didn't make sense, but Poetry said it did, and he tried to prove it to me with a lot of figures.

"How many hours are there in a day?" he asked.

"Twenty-four, of course," I said. "What's that got to do with which way is south?"

But he ignored my remark and asked, "How many figures on a watch?"

"Twelve," I said.

He said with a grin, "Right, Bill Collins. Go to the head of the class. And now answer one more question. If it takes the sun twenty-four hours to complete its one-day cycle, how long would it take it to complete a half day's?"

I must have looked dumb and felt dumber, so he said, still with a mischievous grin on his face, "It would take just twelve hours. Now, from exactly twelve o'clock noon to six o'clock in the evening, the sun would do just one-fourth of its day's work. But that's one half of a twelve-hour day, or one half of the numbers on a watch. So, two hours of a *sun's* day, is equal to one hour of a *watch's* day. Therefore—" Poetry stopped to make the answer of the problem seem very important "—directly south will be just one half of the distance between the twelve on the watch and the shadow of the stick, which lies straight along the length of the hour hand of the watch. See?" he asked.

Imagine anybody seeing through all *that* fog! I didn't see, although I found out afterward that he was right. But I decided then that I had just as well believe that the direction he said was south *was* south as any other, so we jumped up and started in the direction I thought was north, which he said was south.

Every now and then we stopped and looked ahead with my binoculars, hoping to see either the wagon trail or the lake or anything beside trees and trees and trees and fallen logs and underbrush and ferns and all kinds of wild flowers and more trees.

Pretty soon Poetry, who had my binoculars, stopped dead still and exclaimed, "Look! There it is! The trailer! What did I tell you! Come on! Let's hurry up!"

It felt good to have that heavy load of being lost off my chest, so I started to run too.

And then, just as quick, we stopped. For what we'd seen wasn't our nice cream-colored trailer with its silver top but a cream-colored, old-fashioned railroad car! Right out in the middle of the forest!

A railroad car! Had we lost our minds as well as our sense of direction?

6

A railroad coach in the middle of the forest! It couldn't be that, yet it was. We thought at first that there might be a railroad track there, and that we could follow it in the right direction and come to a town and find out where we were.

But there weren't any tracks and hadn't been any, so we were just as lost as we were before. Poetry and I crept up kind of slow at first, until we weren't so afraid, then we walked up to the steps at one end and knocked on the door.

We knocked again, a half-dozen times, thinking maybe somebody had bought the old coach from a railroad company and had moved it into the forest to live in. On the way up north we'd seen some old coaches, just like this one, being lived in by people in some of the towns, and some were even used for roadside lunchrooms.

Nobody answered our knock. So we tried the door to see if it was unlocked, and it was. In a jiffy we were inside, where there were a lot of cobwebs and the old-fashioned cane-backed seats were covered with dust.

The old green blinds at the windows were nearly all pulled down, making it a spooky place and filling our minds with a lot of cobwebbed ideas.

We walked down the length of the coach, feeling all the time as though we ought not to be there because it was somebody else's property. But we kept on exploring it because we liked mysteries so well.

All of a sudden Poetry, who was in the lead, gasped and stopped, and I stopped too, I can tell you, for we saw something black between two of the old seats that were standing back to back.

We could feel our hands trembling on each other's arms, and I could.feel my feet getting ready to run. "Wh-what is it?" I stammered in a scared whisper.

The light wasn't very good, because all the trees outside made so much shade and the blinds were down.

Then Poetry whispered, "Wait," and I waited, listening for all I was worth so that I could run quick if I had to.

Poetry stooped over, and, his being so big, the stooping made him grunt, which sounded like the grunt of an angry Indian. I could feel my hat moving on the top of my red hair, which meant I was really scared.

"It's—well, what in the—" he began. He finished by dragging out something that made a heavy scraping noise on the floor.

We stood looking down at it, feeling foolish but still frightened and as if we were trespassing.

"What is it?" I said, making the nerves in my body stop shaking.

"It's an old suitcase," Poetry's squawky voice said.

Well, we'd read in different newspapers about people who had been murdered, and their bodies had been stuffed into trunks or gunnysacks and things, and I could imagine most anything being in that black suitcase, for it certainly was a big one.

We forgot about being lost for a minute, wanting to solve the mystery.

"Let's open it," I said bravely, "and see who's in it."

Poetry's hand was just reaching down to take hold of the handle when I said that, but it stopped in midair, and he looked at me with the strangest expression on his face.

But Poetry was brave, even when he was scared, and besides, what was there to be scared of? It was just an old dusty suitcase in an abandoned railroad coach!

I never saw any suitcase open the way that one did. It was fastened shut at the bottom rather than at the top—and on the *side* of the bottom at that! But it wasn't locked, so after we'd grunted and pulled a little, it started to open. In another half second it'd have been open if we hadn't been stopped.

Stopped!

We heard a noise at the end of the car where we'd entered.

Then the old sliding door opened with a

rusty squeak that sounded like a screech, and there, standing just inside the doorway, blocking the aisle, was a big bronze American Indian with his war bonnet on and long beads made out of bones hanging around his neck, a brass bracelet on his arm above the elbow, and another around his right wrist. In his hand he held a bow and arrow. There was a scowl on his face.

And standing right beside him was a little boy with black hair hanging down in braids, and his face was as quiet as if he had been a statue.

Well, those things happened in books, but they couldn't happen in real life—not to the Sugar Creek Gang or to any members of it! It couldn't be real. The way everything was all mixed up, it couldn't be anything but a dream. Imagine telling directions by a stick and a watch! Finding a railroad car out in the middle of a forest without any railroad tracks! A big black suitcase that opened at the bottom! And an honest-to-goodness Indian with beads and a war bonnet! In a minute I'd wake up, and I'd be back in my sleeping bag in Poetry's tent.

To make it still more crazy, the little Indian boy didn't have a bow and arrow in *his* hand but a broom! An actual broom and dustpan like the kind my mom used back home. And I tell you, I wished I was back in Sugar Creek territory, or else that I'd wake up. I didn't care which.

Just when my knees started knocking together and I felt myself sinking down toward one of the seats, the big Indian smiled, and his teeth were beautiful and white. When he spoke, it was in good English, or, I should say, American.

"Good afternoon. What are you doing in my church?"

Church! That settled it! It *was* a dream!

Only it wasn't.

"Don't be afraid," the big Indian said. "I won't hurt you. Snow-in-the-Face, here, wanted me to dress up in an old-fashioned Indian outfit and pretend we were the Indians of long ago." He smiled again. "Want to see what is on the inside of the suitcase? You're the boys of the Sugar Creek Gang, who are camping over on the other side of the point, aren't you? I know about you. Snow-in-the-Face and I have been following you, thinking maybe you were lost, and we were going to help you find your way back to camp."

"Wh-who are you?" Poetry stammered.

He was still scared, and I was still dreaming, I thought.

I kept on half thinking that until a minute later, when the big Indian took off his war bonnet, laid it down on a seat, and said, "Here, Snow-in-the-Face, let me have that broom. We'll have to get busy if we want to get our church swept and dusted and ready for the meeting tonight."

Little by little we came to our senses. And this is what we found out. The big Indian was telling the truth. It *was* a church! The members of Santa Claus's church back in Chicago had bought an old railroad car and had it moved out into the forest on the Indian reservation to be used as a church, it being cheaper to buy a church building than to make one.

Snow-in-the-Face and his big brother, whose Indian name was Eagle Eye, were Chippewa Indians. Eagle Eye had become a Christian when he was twelve years old, and he had been away to school—high school and then to a Christian college, where he was studying the Bible and how to be a missionary to his own people. He had just come home for the summer and was going to have meetings in the old railroad coach. The members of Santa's church in Chicago were going to support him as their own missionary.

If every church in the world would support just one missionary, the rest of the world would get converted quick, I'll bet. Poetry figured it up once, and he says it's so, and Little Jim wishes it was.

Well, it was like getting out of a whirlwind alive to come out of all that tangled-up mystery without getting hurt. Camp was just on the other side of the point from us, Eagle Eye said, and he'd drive us around there after a while if we'd help him clean up his church. The old wagon trail was just south of us a little way.

"Like to see the suitcase?" Eagle Eye asked again, and he lifted it and carried it down to the other end of the coach, where there was a little platform. He opened it up, and it wasn't a suitcase at all but a little folding organ, with keys and pedals and a rack for a hymnbook and everything.

It didn't take us long to finish the work, and then we drove back to camp in Eagle Eye's kind of old car, which was parked the distance of about two blocks away. We got there just about the same time the fishermen came in with a big string of walleyed pike.

I took out my watch to see what time it was, and Poetry, who was in a very good humor, looked at me and said, "What direction is it?"

"Five minutes after south," I said, grinning, feeling better than I had for a long time.

Just that minute Santa and Dragonfly and Circus and Little Jim came driving into camp, and for the first time Snow-in-the-Face smiled. He climbed out of Eagle Eye's rickety old car and shuffled over to the other one to get a sack of stick candy that Santa had brought for him, and which he must have been expecting. He and Santa seemed to be very good friends.

We heard someone calling us from the dock about that time. It was Tom Till, standing up in the boat, which was in very shallow water, and holding up the biggest string of the biggest fish I'd ever seen in my life, making that little old nine-inch bass that Dragonfly had caught in Sugar Creek last summer seem very small. Very, very small.

7

Not only was there a big string of big fish, but there was one stringer on which there was just one fish that weighed twelve pounds!

Whew! That northern pike had a mouth almost large enough to get a boy's head into it, and it had sharp teeth like a saw's teeth. Its nose was long and ridiculous looking. I couldn't help but wish I'd caught it myself, so I could have had my picture taken with it, as Big Jim was having done to him right that minute, for it was he who had caught it.

As I told you, Santa had gone to town to get some minnows—which they keep there in a live bait store—so that the rest of the gang could go fishing when the first boatful of fishermen came back. So now it was our turn, but there were still too many of us. It wasn't any fun to try to troll with more than three in a boat at one time, because the lines would get in each other's way.

Finally Barry rented another boat from the boat livery at the resort, so all the rest of us could go at the same time. Santa Claus took Circus and me in his boat, and Barry took Dragonfly and Little Jim and Poetry. Little Jim said he wouldn't fish but would just go along for the ride, and he'd holler every time anybody caught a fish.

That made Poetry say, "Then we don't want you in our boat, 'cause we don't want you to be yelling every minute! Go over and get into Bill's boat, so you can keep nice and quiet!"

I had my dad's light steel pole with a reel and all the latest fishing equipment, although I didn't know how to use it very well. It was fun learning how, though.

Santa showed me the best way to do it, and we were soon out on the lake, put-putting over the waves. Riding in a boat on a lake felt like sitting in Mom's favorite rocking chair at home, except that the boat didn't only rock backward and forward but sidewise and every other direction, whichever way the boat turned. Sometimes it seemed it was rocking in a half-dozen directions at once.

Trolling was great fun. The lake wasn't rough, but even if it had been we wouldn't have been afraid, because we were all wearing our life preservers. Our parents had bought them for us, because the flood in Sugar Creek last spring made them cautious. The vests were kind of awkward, but we got used to them, knowing that if a big storm should come up, or if anything did happen—such as a boat turning over—we'd all float in the water with our heads up, and if the wind would keep on blowing we'd drift to shore somewhere.

I'm sorry to have to say that we caught only about five fish on our trip out, although I could hear Little Jim and everybody else in the other boat making an awful noise. Their boat had gone on ahead of us and was around on the other side of the point, so we could hear them but not see them.

On the way back, I kept feeling disappointed because we had only five walleyed pike, none of which was more than fifteen inches long, and the others would surely have almost a boatful by all the noise they were making. But when they came in, they had only two or three big rock bass, and Poetry's line was all tangled up and broken, he having lost the hook and leader and a fish that must have weighed twenty pounds, he said.

There was plenty of excitement in that boat though. Everybody was talking at once, telling how big the fish was that got away, and Poetry was still shaking from the excitement of having had it on his line and almost but not quite landing it.

Poetry carried his pole and tangled-up line sadly toward camp, with the rest of us following along behind, feeling sorry for him.

"I tell you it was *that* long!" he said, measuring off about three feet on the pole, "and it weighed twenty pounds!"

"How much?" Big Jim asked, grunting and holding up his own twelve-pound fish and admiring it.

"Twenty!" said Poetry again. "Why, it felt like a great big dog on the other end of the line."

Then Big Jim laughed and said, "Ha! If mine had gotten away, I'll bet it would have weighed twenty pounds too, but on the scales it only weighed twelve."

Poetry looked at him disgustedly and then walked away and began to untangle his fishing line. I went along with him to help him, and Dragonfly came too to keep us company.

Pretty soon we heard Barry calling for all of us to come and have our first lesson in cleaning fish.

I didn't want to go at first. If there was anything in the world I hated worse than hoeing potatoes or doing dishes, it was cleaning fish.

But it was as easy as eating blackberry pie, the way Barry cleaned those fish. He didn't even scrape the scales off. He just laid the fish one at a time on a flat board on the table. Then, beginning at the tail, with a long sharp knife he just sliced that fish right up along the center and came out at the gills, and there was a nice piece of fish steak, which restaurants call *fillet of fish.*

Then he turned over the half of the fish that was left and did the same thing. He sliced all the way up, right along the edge of the backbone, coming out just below the gills. And quicker'n nothing there was another snow-white steak. Each steak still had the skin and scales on one side.

Then Barry picked up the fish's head, and all the insides and the backbone and the fins and tail were still fastened to it. He dropped it into a big paper sack. *He didn't even have to touch the insides!* Which is why I'd never liked to clean fish.

I forgot to say that he'd held the fish with one hand and used the knife with the other, and he had a dry cloth to keep the slimy fish from sliding out of his grasp.

Well, there was nothing to do now but to take off the scales and the skin, which was as easy as peeling a banana. All Barry did was lay the steak on the flat board with the scales side *down*. Then he caught hold of a tiny piece of the tail end and slid the sharp-bladed knife back and forth as if it was a saw, pressing down all the time. And in about four seconds there was a nice piece of steak, white on both sides with no bones in it except the ribs.

It didn't take long to clean them all and to put them on ice in the icebox. Then we had supper and another campfire meeting, and it was time to go to bed again.

For tomorrow Barry had planned what is called a first-aid hike, which real Boy Scouts are always taking. We'd been up there for three days now, and nothing very exciting had happened, that is, no real adventure, except being almost scared to death in the railroad car.

Before going to sleep that night, I thought cheerfully of what was going to happen the next day. We'd get a chance to see what the north was really like. We'd never had a first-aid hike, although I suppose Big Jim had, because he was a Boy Scout; and, of course, Barry had.

Tomorrow! I was sleeping in Poetry's tent, with Little Jim lying right beside me in his own sleeping bag. He was already breathing away noisily, the way a boy breathes when he's asleep. Breathing like that even helps a person go to sleep when he's got what is called insomnia—if he just pretends he's asleep and starts to breathe kind of lazy-like and with a noise that sounds like my dad's handsaw cutting through a board.

For just one minute I stuck my head out the tent flap to look up at the stars and at the little grains of light I liked to imagine were sprinkling down. There was a big yellow moon just pushing its head up out of the lake away out there where the sky and the lake were fastened together.

That moon was the same moon that was just coming up along Sugar Creek too, I thought, and I wondered how it could do it. I also thought that maybe that very minute down in Sugar Creek territory, my great big dad and my very kindhearted mom might be sitting out on our side porch, holding hands, each one in a chair close to the other one.

And maybe Dad would call Mom one of his favorite names for her and say, "I wonder if our Billy-boy is lonesome for his parents." And Mom would giggle a little and say, "Sure he is. There isn't a boy in the world that likes his parents better than our Bill." Then Mom and Dad would stand up and look at the same moon I was looking at, and then they'd go in the house and go to bed.

Well, it had been an exciting day, and we were so tired that we slept like eight logs being sawed with noisy saws, which means we snored.

8

It was Poetry's almost-and-yet-not-quite catching that big fish that got us into trouble near the last of the first week. He couldn't get over the fact that he'd lost it, and he made up his mind that before the camping trip was over he was going back there and catch that fish, if it was the last thing he ever did. He told me about it, and he talked about it every day.

But as I said, the very next day after Poetry had lost the fish, Barry had planned a first-aid hike. We'd be gone all morning and wouldn't get back in time to make dinner, he said, so we'd put our fish dinner on to cook right away.

We'd been cooking nearly all our meals on the gas stove in the trailer, but today's dinner was to be cooked in the ground. I'd never heard of such a thing, but I was willing to do my part. Barry put us all to work—after breakfast and after we'd had a little talk from the Bible by Santa, who came over just in time.

My job to help get the dinner ready was to dig a hole in the ground eighteen inches deep and the same distance in every other direction. I got a shovel from the resort and went to work.

Poetry and Little Jim and Circus were sent to gather stones, a couple of bucketfuls, enough to completely line the hole. The idea looked silly, but Barry told us to do it, so do it we did.

With a grunt, Poetry set his rocks down beside me and said, "Be sure you dig it far enough south."

Pretty soon the hole was finished and lined with rocks, each one pushed up close against the other. Big Jim put in kindling wood and dry twigs, making a pile about two feet high and stacking the sticks in a crisscross style. Then he started a fire, which we let burn for a whole hour, while we did different things around camp, waiting for all the wood to burn up. Barry sent us after basswood leaves and wild grape leaves and leaves from sassafras shrubs, and we even got some lettuce leaves, which we found in the icebox.

"All right, Bill, bring your shovel," Barry called, which I did. "Now scoop out all the ashes and live coals and pile them here. Circus, get a bucketful of sand, quick. Dragonfly, get those old burlap sacks there by the trailer door and soak them in the lake and bring them here as wet as you can."

It still looked very strange to us, but we obeyed anyway, and soon I had all the coals scooped out, leaving nothing in the hole but hot stones. Barry lined them with the green leaves, and then quicker than anything he put in about a dozen big fish steaks right in the center of the hole. All around the fish he put potatoes and corn on the cob and carrots. On top of that he spread more green leaves and more stones.

Then he laid on the soaking-wet burlap sacks, just as Circus came puffing up with a pail of sand from the beach. Barry made me scoop some more sandy soil on top of that, making a little mound.

Well, to me it didn't make sense. It looked like the end of a funeral, with the fish being the corpse. All we needed now was a tombstone, and it would all be over.

So I said to Poetry, calling him by his real name, which is Leslie Thompson, "Leslie," I said solemnly, "go get your fishing pole, the one you caught the twenty-pound fish with, and set it up for a tombstone."

Which made him turn red in the face, and he said, "Just you wait and see. I'm going to learn *how* to fish. And before we go back to Sugar Creek, I'll catch that big old northern if it's the last thing I ever do," not knowing that it would come mighty near to *being* the last thing he'd ever do. Why, if it hadn't been for—but that's too far ahead of the story. I'll get to it pretty soon, though. First, let me tell you about our first-aid hike.

With the "funeral" over, Barry handed me a white envelope, saying, "You're the guinea pig today."

You see, a first-aid hike is one in which some boy of the gang or Scout patrol is given an envelope with instructions in it, telling him what kind of an accident he is to pretend he has had. He doesn't know himself, until he opens the envelope, just what is supposed to have happened to him. He walks along ahead of the gang, starting five minutes before they do. Then after five minutes maybe, no matter where he is, he stops, opens the envelope, and reads the instructions. Whatever they say, he does.

Sometimes he has to pretend he's fallen out of a tree and broken his arm or leg; sometimes he has fainted, or fallen into the lake and drowned. The rest of the gang come along, find out what's happened, and administer first aid. It's good sport and good training.

We were just ready to start when we had a case of real first aid to take care of. Poetry had reached up under his shirt to scratch his side and felt something funny there, so he jerked back his shirttail and looked. And there was a little wood tick sticking headfirst right into his side. In fact, that tick's head was completely buried.

Now, I'd read about wood ticks in a book, and they're dangerous if the head gets left in when you pull them off. You might even get a fever and be sick.

It didn't take long to take care of the tick, though. Big Jim knew exactly what to do, and Barry let him do it. He sent Dragonfly after a match in the trailer. Then he lit the match and let it burn until there was a red-hot coal on the end. Then, quick as a flash, he touched the hot end of the match to the tail of that wood tick, being very careful not to touch Poetry himself.

Wow! You should have seen that little flat rascal of a wood tick wiggle and squirm and come backing out of Poetry's side the way our old horse Jim backs out of his stall at home, or else like my dad's car does when he backs it out of the garage and is in a hurry to get to town—although Big Jim did have to use another match to make him back all the way out.

And now for the hike. I took the white envelope and started off down the lakeshore, only to be stopped by Poetry, who yelled, "Hey, what direction are you going?"

"Keep still!" I yelled back at him and went on, minding my own business, wondering all the time what was written on the paper in the envelope.

I was supposed to walk along the shore, Barry had told me, until I came to where the big point of land starts to go out into the lake. Then I was to keep on following the shoreline until I came to the boat belonging to Eagle Eye and his brother, Snow-in-the-Face. There I should stop and read my instructions.

So I started out. It was a great morning, with the lake looking like a big silvery-blue mirror with live wrinkles on its face. Already I could see the point of land, jutting out maybe a half mile into the lake, something like a long neck without any head.

That was where Poetry and I had been lost that other day before we knew very much about the territory up there. And that explains why we could hear a loon first on one side of us and then the other. There had been two loons, and they were hollering to each other across the neck of land, like two boys hollering to each other across a schoolyard.

On the other side of the neck was a sandbar, and nearby were schools and schools of walleye that liked to chase after minnows. On the other side, too, was a long shoreline of bulrushes where, in different places, some big northern pike lay in hiding on the bottom of the lake, waiting for a live breakfast or a live dinner or supper to come swimming along. Then they would shoot like torpedoes under the water straight toward that dinner.

If that live dinner happened to have a hook in it with a boy on the other end of the line, the northern pike himself would turn into dinner for a hungry boy.

While walking along, I thought that I would like to be a fish, living down in the interesting underwater world, with the strange-looking other fish all around me. I'd go on an exploring trip, down, down, down to the very bottom of the lake. Maybe I'd organize a special gang of fish and have a lot of fun. There'd be a big northern pike and a little northern pike, a fat sunfish and an acrobatic bass, a very walleyed pike, and a red-finned, spotted muskellunge, which would be me with my red hair and freckles.

Just then I heard a motorboat go put-putting by on the lake, and I knew it was mail time at camp. In my mind I could see the gang all running down the long deck toward the mailbox at the end to see if there were any letters from home.

Pretty soon I came to the white boat that belonged to Eagle Eye and Snow-in-the-Face. There I stopped, tore open the envelope, and read the note inside, which was written on a typewriter. "Dear Guinea Pig," it said,

Find south by using your watch, then walk straight west until you come out on the other side of the point, where you will find a sandbar willow, growing right at the edge of the water. There you are supposed to drown yourself, only please don't do it.

Wait in the shade of the willow until you hear us coming, then slide off into the shallow water and call for help. Play dead until we get to you, and for five minutes after we get there, until we've restored your breathing by artificial respiration. We'll let you know when you're alive again.

I finished reading the note, put it back into its envelope, shoved it into my pocket, took out my watch, and picked up a little stick about the size of a match. It was just half past nine, I noticed, not nearly as late as I'd thought it was.

I laid the watch down on the palm of my hand, set up the stick on the outside of the rim, and turned the watch around until the shadow of the stick fell straight along the hour hand. South, I knew, would be just halfway between the point of the hour hand and the figure twelve on the dial.

Anybody could find west if he knew which way south was, so I grinned and started west. I walked along, feeling happy, thinking of a lot of cheerful things, glad I was alive and remembering some of the important things Barry or Santa had been telling us in the campfire talks. I was beginning to get hungry too, thinking about the buried dinner under the old wet burlap sacks back at camp.

Yes sir, I tell you it was great to be alive. A rabbit jumped up—a little reddish-brown one —and scooted across in front of me. A crazy loon let out a weird noise from the lake. Another rabbit jumped out just then and started to run, going straight west, the same direction I was going.

Or was it north? All of a sudden I had a funny feeling, and every direction I looked was the same direction, and there were trees and trees and more trees. It was just as it had been that other time when Poetry and I had been lost.

But I didn't worry, because I knew how to find directions now myself. I took out my watch and— would you believe this?—it was still half past nine! My watch had stopped running and had maybe been stopped for a long time! *Why, it ought to be almost eleven by now,* I thought; and if I could have told the time with my stomach, it would have been way after twelve, I was so hungry.

I stood still, thinking. We must have put the dinner in its grave about ten o'clock. Then Poetry had had to be operated on. Hm! *Let me see,* I thought. *Yes, it ought to be about eleven by now.*

But that would change the directions all around! It meant that I hadn't been going in the right direction at all. I might miss the willow tree when I got there.

Anyway, I set my watch forward to eleven o'clock, wound it, and found south again. Then I started out in the direction I thought I was supposed to go, feeling funny and wondering, *What if I get lost again!*

Barry had said in his talk last night, "See there, boys? That's why we have to have the Bible, which is God's Word, to show us the right direction to go. Nobody would know right from wrong, or how to live at all, or how to go to heaven, if we didn't have this compass."

Then he had held up the Bible for us to see, and I had reached into my vest pocket, where I always kept my New Testament, and felt proud to think that my parents knew enough to buy me one and teach me to read it.

I kept on walking, knowing I was going close to right and that sooner or later I'd get across the neck of the forest, which I did. In about three minutes more I heard the washing of waves against a shore, and there was the lake and the sandbar and the willow, near the water's edge.

I waded out through the soft white sand and lay down in the shade of the little tree, wondering why the shade should be on the south side of the tree at noon when it was supposed to be on the north.

Oh, well, I thought, *I never was very good at* feeling *directions.* So I quit worrying about it. It didn't matter how I felt. South was south, and nobody could change it, just like the ·Bible, which says, "Believe in the Lord Jesus, and you will be saved," and that settles it!

We boys liked Barry Boyland, and we thought our parents were the wisest parents in the world to give us that kind of vacation.

Pretty soon the gang would be coming to bring me back to life again, so I lay there thinking and imagining what if I *was* dead! I guess my mom and dad and little Charlotte Ann would be lonesome without me, and I'd be lonesome for them.

First they'd take the red-haired, freckled-faced body that I used to live in out to the cemetery behind our church and bury it. And everybody would cry and cry and feel very sad, Mom and Dad most of all. And we wouldn't be able to have any more of our three-cornered hugs—I think maybe I'd miss that most of all.

Maybe someday up there, I'd walk down a quiet sort of lane, with a lot of birds singing in the trees on each side, and there upon a pretty little hill would be a kind of oldish-looking cabin, all fixed up for Old Man Paddler to live in when he came. Because I don't think he'd want to live in a big fine house. He'd rather, if it cost anything to make it, have Jesus save the money to help the missionaries preach the gospel, or else help some poor boys get a good chance in life down on the earth.

I might even walk up to the oldish-looking cabin some morning and look after the flowers for him, so that when he got there, everything'd be just like he'd like to have it. Then I'd get a drink at his spring if I was thirsty, although Sylvia's dad says we won't ever get thirsty in heaven. Maybe the Bible means, though, that a boy can always have all the water he wants.

Anyway, maybe Jesus Himself would come

walking along, with the scars still showing in His hands where He'd suffered on the cross for everybody. He'd smile and lay one of His hands on my head and say, "Thank you, Bill. Whatever you do for others who love Me, you do for Me." And maybe He'd give me the same kind of hug my dad does.

Well, that's as far as I got to think just then, because all of a sudden I felt something cold touch my nose. I opened my eyes quick. And there was a little blackish-green turtle with silly, blinking eyes looking right straight into mine, not more than a few inches away. In fact, I had to look cross-eyed to see him, he was so close. I knew right away that I wasn't in heaven.

I'd seen little turtles like this one before, down along Sugar Creek. They were always swimming and diving around in the water, and sometimes they'd crawl up on the land and travel to different places. Turtles even migrate, the way birds do, although they don't move in such big companies as birds or grasshoppers.

And that reminds me—when Old Man Paddler was a boy, grasshoppers used to be so thick sometimes that when they'd fly, or migrate, from one part of the country to another, they'd actually hide the sun like a big cloud, and it'd be almost dark on the earth.

Well, sometimes when turtles shuffle around up on the shore, they try to cross the road, and they get run over, not having as much sense as a boy, who looks both ways before he starts and waits if he doesn't have time enough to get across.

This little guy was as surprised as I was, and he didn't seem to like me any better than I did him. He turned around as quick as anything, scrambled away toward the willow tree, and started headfirst into a patch of grass, a little like a wood tick squirming headfirst into a boy's side, carrying his bony house with him as turtles do. I'd hate to have to carry a house with me wherever I went, although I suppose if it was a part of me, I wouldn't mind so much.

Just that minute I heard the gang coming. I rolled over a couple of times and went *kersplash* into the water, screamed a wild scream for help, splashed around a little and sank to the bottom, the water being only about eight inches deep. I lay on my back with my face and nose sticking up like a turtle's nose when it's in the water and just looking around, only I kept my eyes shut.

Then I screamed another blood-curdling scream and kept on lying still with my eyes shut.

I could hear footsteps running across the sand, *squash, swish, crunchety, crunch-crunch-crunch,* the kind of noise a boy makes when he is eating dry crackers.

I kept on keeping my eyes shut and my lips too, trying hard not to grin—and thinking of how cold the water was, and that kept me from smiling.

Then for a fraction of a second, I opened my eyes and shut them quick. Would you believe it? I couldn't believe it myself at first. It wasn't the gang at all but little black-haired, black-eyed Snow-in-the-Face.

9

I never saw anything look stranger than Snow-in-the-Face's face when he was looking down at me, lying there in the water. He was really worried.

He couldn't talk American very well, which meant that at home his parents talked Chippewa. He had strawberry stains on his lips, which I was pleased to see because it meant that there was a patch of wild berries around there somewhere, which I could find sometime, when I came back to life.

Quick as a flash he stooped down and caught hold of me to try to lift me out of the water. He was only a little smaller than I was, but he was very strong. Of course, I couldn't let him pull me out, because any minute the gang might come along, so I groaned and fell back limp.

"What's the matter?" he grunted. "Back hurt?"

"No," I moaned, "I'm all right—*oooh!*"

"Leg broke?"

I shook my head.

He was down in the sand at the very edge of the water, trying to get his hands under my neck, but I wouldn't let him.

"Where hurt?" he asked anxiously. "I go get Eagle Eye. Take you home."

"No, no!" I groaned. "Leave me here. I-I'm sick!" *There*, I thought. *That'll make him quit try-*

ing to pull me out of the water. For pulling me out of the water was the gang's job, if they ever came. Poor little guy! He was so sorry for me.

"Maybe stomach hurt? Too many strawberries? You very sick," Snow-in-the-Face said. "I get Eagle Eye quick!" He scrambled to his feet, getting sand in my face and eyes at the same time.

"*Stop!*" I yelled. "I'm not sick. I-I'm *dead!* I drowned a few minutes ago!"

He stopped then, with the strangest expression on his face. Then he grunted and said, "White boy crazy in the red head!" He started to go again.

But just that minute there was a noise up the shore like more boys eating crackers. I looked, and there was the gang coming toward me—Big Jim and Little Jim and Circus and Poetry and Dragonfly and Little Tom Till. And Barry Boyland.

The way Barry gave orders was great. He made his voice sound very authoritative, as though I had really drowned and had to be brought back to life.

"Quick!" he commanded. "Poetry, go telephone for Dr. Dragonfly. Circus, you run back to camp for a blanket." (Except that the blanket was already there. They'd brought it along with them to wrap me in.)

Snow-in-the-Face piped up and said, "I go get blanket. Not far away."

But they wouldn't let him.

The next five minutes there was a lot of pretended excitement. I had found the wrong sandbar and the wrong willow tree, which is why the gang hadn't found me sooner. If they hadn't seen Snow-in-the-Face, I might have had to wait still longer.

The gang pulled me out of the water and started working to give artificial respiration, which is what they do with a boy who has quit breathing but whose heart has not stopped beating. And even when the heart *has* stopped beating, they do it sometimes just in case it *really* hasn't. Maybe the boy's soul is still in him, not having gone to heaven yet—if he was a *saved* boy, which means if he had believed on the Lord Jesus as his own personal Savior.

I tried to imagine how I looked lying there as pale as a ripe tomato, with my hair all mussed up. I could have been called "Dirt-in-the-Face." Thinking that almost made me start to grin.

"Start to work quick!" Barry commanded. "Waste no time carrying him anywhere! Save the seconds, and you have a better chance of saving his life!" That sounded sensible and is what real Scout leaders teach.

I guess Barry had explained to the gang ahead of time just what to do and had appointed Poetry and Big Jim to work on me. They flopped me over in the sand, stomach down, with my right arm extending above my head. They bent my left arm at the elbow and slipped it under my face, which was turned sideways, letting me have the back of my left hand and the crook of the arm for a pillow. This kept my nose and mouth out of the sand so I could breathe.

Then Big Jim went down on his knees, straddling my right leg. All of a sudden I felt the palms of his big hands on the small of my back at the bottom of my ribs, and it seemed the whole weight of his body was pushing down on my back, squeezing all the wind out of me and making me grunt, which made Poetry say, "He's alive, all right," but Big Jim shushed him.

Then Big Jim's hands were off again—then on again. First he'd press down with all his strength, then he'd straighten up, wait two seconds, and forward he'd come again and press down with all his strength. When you do that to a boy or anybody else who has drowned, you might start his lungs working again and save his life.

Up, down, up, down. Big Jim was awfully heavy, and I wished they'd hurry up and tell me I was alive, so I could rest. I felt sorry for all the people in the world who had the kind of infantile paralysis that paralyzes what are called the "respiratory muscles," so they can't breathe.

Up, down, up, down. And I wished Dr. Dragonfly would hurry up and come.

I could hear Big Jim breathing hard, getting tired himself. I opened my eyes, and Snow-in-the-Face was still looking worried in the face. I'll bet there were a lot of twisted-up thoughts wiggling around in his little head. Of course, when I saw him looking at me, I shut my eyes again quick.

"All right, Big Jim," Barry said, "let Poetry relieve you," meaning "let Poetry take your place so you can rest." There was only a second before Poetry's big hands were pressing down with all his might, like a ton of soft bricks crushing the life out of me. I knew that if Poetry didn't bring me back to life nobody would—or else he'd be sure to kill me.

"Ugh!" I grunted. "Not so heavy!"

Then I heard a sound like more crackers being eaten. I opened my eyes, and there was Dr. Dragonfly, with a forked stick for a doctor's stethoscope.

"He's breathing," Poetry said, puffing away with his own breath.

I took another quick peep through my thick red eyelashes and saw Dragonfly with his stethoscope leaning over me. Little Tom stooped down and stuck an open bottle of ammonia under my nose, which Circus had just given him, and which didn't smell very good.

"Put the hot water bottle here," Dr. Dragonfly said. "His heart is still beating but very slowly."

Somebody pushed a big flat rock, which was supposed to be a hot water bottle, up against my legs, and all the time Poetry was giving me artificial respiration every five seconds, which is fifteen times a minute. Or is it twelve?

"How is he, doctor?" Barry asked soberly.

"Another hour may bring him to life," Dragonfly said. "It sometimes takes two hours. Nobody ought to give up until they've tried for two hours, unless there is a doctor there to tell you he is dead."

Another hour! It seemed they'd worked on me for three hours already. I opened my eyes a little again and saw Little Jim sitting down under the willow with the black-and-green turtle on his lap, not paying any attention to us. He had his knife out of his pocket and was scratching away on the green roof of the turtle's house. *What in the world?* I thought.

Pretty soon Dragonfly listened again to my heart and stuck a feather in front of my nose and mouth to see if the fuzzy feather would move a little and I was breathing, which I was and which it did.

But Dragonfly was having a good time. He straightened up and said sadly, sounding just like a doctor saying something important, "The boy is dead. There's no use to continue."

Well, that was enough for me. I tell you, I came to life pretty quick, rolled over, shoved Poetry off into the water, and sat up, disgusted with everybody but very much alive.

Snow-in-the-Face looked at me and at all of us and then grunted, "All white boys crazy." He started off on the run across the sand toward a little forest path that would take him back to his home.

I scrambled to my feet, covered with sand, which stuck to my clothes because they were wet, shook myself the way a dog does when it comes out of the water, and said, "I'm *hungry!*" yelling the last word.

Just then Little Jim scrambled to *his* feet, still holding the turtle, whose legs were sticking out from under its roof and were moving the way Charlotte Ann's do when she's being held in somebody's arms and doesn't want to be but wants to be put down.

I'd supposed, of course, that Little Jim had been scratching his initials on the turtle's back, but he wasn't.

"Look!" he said to all of us, holding it up

for us to see. And there on the turtle's bony back was printed:

JOHN 3:16

Which goes to show that that little fellow was always thinking the right kind of thoughts.

"Let's take him back to camp," Dr. Dragonfly said, looking at the turtle, "and perform a surgical operation."

"Nothing doing," Little Jim objected. "Watch!"

He walked over to the lake, stooped down, and set the wriggling turtle in the sand right at the water's edge. Talk about something being in a hurry! You should have seen that turtle beat it! In a flash he was gone, right into the water, all of his little legs paddling fiercely, straight to the bottom of the lake, which was as clear as drinking water.

And just that minute Little Jim said, quoting from the Bible, "'Go therefore and make disciples of all the nations, baptizing them in the name of the Father and the Son and the Holy Spirit.'"

Someday, I thought, *somebody may find that turtle, and read the writing on the roof of its house, and look it up in the Bible, and believe on Jesus Christ and get everlasting life, just like it says.*

Hm, I wonder how many people in the world are as interested in spreading the Gospel as that grand Little Jim guy of the Sugar Creek Gang? Not very many, I'll bet, or there wouldn't be so many boys in the world whose parents aren't Christians like Little Jim's and mine, and some of the rest of the Sugar Creek Gang's, Dragonfly's and Little Tom's parents being the only ones who weren't Christians.

10

Two surprises were waiting for me when we got back to camp. The first was a letter from the folks at home, and the other was what we found when we dug up our dinner.

I think the rest of the gang was as hungry as I was, because it took us only a little while to get back, not nearly as long as it took me to get to the sandbar in the first place.

As soon as I'd changed clothes, Big Jim said, "Bill, there was a letter for you. We left it in the box."

Dr. Dragonfly went along with me out to the end of the long dock to the mailbox, the dock being long because the water near the shore was too shallow for a motorboat to run in.

Sure enough, there was a letter from home in my mom's handwriting, telling about different things, such as Mixy's kittens, blackberry pie for dinner that day, and Big Bob Till's hoeing potatoes for my dad for two days and eating dinner at our house.

Then Mom added some very unnecessary advice about me being sure to have good manners at the table, being courteous to everybody, and not to forget my New Testament. Imagine Mom being afraid I'd not have good manners away from home! I always had good manners when I was in other people's houses or with other people. I was even beginning to have good manners at home.

Then there was a note from Charlotte Ann, who couldn't write by herself but had scribbled and scratched with a pencil the way a baby does when her mother holds her hand for her:

Dear big brother Bill,

Mom and Dad and I had a three-cornered hug this morning, with Dad holding me in one arm and Mom in the other, and with me in between. Then Dad and Mom sat down with Mom holding me, and Dad read a verse or two out of the Bible and talked about you and me. Then he and Mom bowed their heads and shut their eyes and talked to Somebody about you and me and each other. I think I saw tears in Mom's eyes when they quit talking about us, and Mom said to Dad, "I hope Bill remembers to wear his life preserver whenever he goes out in the boat up there." So maybe you'd better be sure to do it.

With love,
Charlotte Ann

I finished reading the letter, feeling something like a big strawberry lodged in my throat. Thinking about the strawberry made me hungry, so Dr. Dragonfly and I went racing up the dock to where the gang was digging up our dinner—the raw fish and potatoes and carrots and raw corn on the cob, I thought.

But I thought wrong!

First, Barry took off the sand and dirt, being careful not to dig too deep. Then he lifted off the rocks and the burlap sacks, and there underneath were the leaves, and inside that— yum! Yum! I could smell that dinner ten feet away!

Barry set everything out on a homemade table in the shade of a big balsam tree, so each of us could walk around cafeteria style and help himself. But first, we all stood around the table, with the steam from the potatoes and fish making us so hungry we could hardly stand it, and Barry started a little song, which went:

"We thank Thee, Lord, for this, our food,
For life and health and every good . . ."

All of us joined in, even Tom Till, whose voice wasn't even worth mentioning, because it stayed on the same pitch all the way through. But Circus's high soprano switched off into a tenor that was beautiful and as clear as a dinner bell.

I opened my eyes, which I wasn't supposed to, and saw Circus's brown curly hair looking like it had that night when he went lickety-sizzle down the aisle of the big evangelistic tent in our town—and his dad got saved the same night.

Pretty soon we were sitting cross-legged, or squatting, or half lying down in different places, eating the best dinner I ever had in my life. You should have seen the letter I wrote to the folks about it.

I put what is called a "P.S." on the end of the letter and said,

Dear Charlotte Ann:

Sure, I'll remember to wear my life preserver. Think I want to drown in the lake when I have the grandest little baby sister in the world? With ears that look like halves of dried peaches glued onto the sides of her little round head, which looks like a pinkish-white pumpkin with dimples and smiles? Tell Mom not to worry. Barry Boyland is letting me learn how to run a little outboard motor, and sometimes I go lickety-sizzle up and down the shore, when the water is not rough. But even when the water is quiet, we wear our life preservers, because it's safer to have them on and because we like to *feel* safe. Even if we did have an accident and suddenly found ourselves in the water, we wouldn't drown but would float along, shoulders up, and be perfectly safe. So, little black-haired, rose-petal-lipped, grand little wriggler, don't worry about your freckle-faced big brother, Bill. I'll be seeing you in about ten days.

It certainly was great running a motorboat all by myself. It was the easiest thing in the world to do, because the directions telling how to run it were printed right on the top of the gasoline tank. Of course, I made a few mistakes learning how, but after that, with Poetry and Dragonfly or some of the rest of the gang in the boat with me, I'd go whizzing out across the water.

The days flew along with plenty of fun and excitement nearly every day—and with all of us learning a lot of important things from the Bible, because there was a class every morning for half an hour, with Barry teaching us or maybe Santa or Mrs. Santa.

We had fish to eat at least once a day, for once in our lives getting all the fish we wanted. The last week we planned to catch a lot of big ones to take home, packed in ice, to show the folks that our fish stories were true. And all the time, Poetry kept hoping he'd hook the big twenty-pounder he had lost that one day. The rest of the gang hoped they'd catch it too, but none of them did.

Along about the end of the first week, a stray kitten came into camp and meowed as if it had lost its mother, so Little Jim began to feed it fish and milk and different things, whatever it'd eat. It was called a tiger kitten, having stripes on it like a tiger has, and it had the pleasantest face.

"I'll bet it's lost," Little Jim said in Little Jim's way of saying things like that.

And right away I knew we'd have to have another member in the Sugar Creek Gang, at least until time to go back home.

At first, we could hardly walk anywhere for that kitten getting in the way and wanting to lean up against our legs.

"Do you know why it does that?" Little Jim asked me one day.

"Why it does what?" I asked.

And he said, "Why it leans up against your legs and pushes itself slowly past, then turns around and walks past your legs again, all the time kind of half leaning up against you."

"No," I said. "Why does it do it?"

"'Cause," Little Jim said, grinning, "it likes to be petted so well, and it can't wait for you to do it, so it *makes* you pet it. It makes it just as happy as if you were stroking it with your hand. Kittens have to have lots of love."

I looked at his big round eyes, and, say, that little guy didn't even know he'd said something that my dad would say was "very philosophical."

Before the second week was gone, Little Jim liked the kitten so well that we knew we'd never be able to go home without it. And yet, who wanted any more cats around Sugar Creek? I knew that Little Jim's parents wouldn't want another cat around the house, and the Collins family certainly didn't need any more.

It was still the first week, though, so I mustn't get ahead of the story. Pretty soon it was the first Sunday, and all the gang dressed up in their Sunday clothes, and we drove into town to church.

This church was just like any ordinary church, except that about one-fourth of the worshipers were American Indians. The gang and their friends sat in a row by themselves. Sitting right next to me was little Snow-in-the-Face, and on the other side of him was his mother.

Santa sang a solo, which was the best I'd ever heard.

While he was singing, I looked for a minute at Circus, and his eyes were shining. He'd never heard anybody who could sing so well and who was a born-again Christian at the same time— and who was always trying to get somebody else to become one. Circus's fists were all doubled up, and he was almost trembling. I could see that he liked Santa almost as well as we all liked Barry Boyland—and wanted to be the same kind of man they both were.

After church, when Circus and I were standing out by the car watching the people go home, Circus looked at me and said, "When I get big, I'm going to be a pastor of a church in a big city and sing and preach both." Then he climbed into the backseat of the car, took out his knife, opened the blade, and looked at it as if it was a very interesting knife, blinking his eyes a little like they had dust in them.

After dinner, we all changed clothes—in fact, we changed clothes first. And after we'd had a little nap, which is good for boys on Sunday afternoons, if you can get them to take it, we all hiked over to the railroad coach near the Indian reservation, where Eagle Eye was conducting a Sunday school.

On the way over we passed by the place

where the neck of the forest is fastened onto its body, and Poetry and I dropped behind the gang a little and planned an early morning fishing trip around the point, with our minds all made up to catch that big fish.

"Look there!" Poetry said, pointing out across the lake. Its waves were moving like lazy boys hoeing potatoes, not caring whether they moved at all. The whole lake, with the sun shining down on it, looked like a big blue desert with a gang of white seagulls tumbling around in the air above it.

Poetry had just started to say, "'O beautiful for spacious skies—'" when we heard a twig snap behind us, and it was Dr. Dragonfly. He'd heard what we'd been planning about the fishing trip early the next morning.

"I'm going too," he announced without asking us if we wanted him.

"Nothing doing," Poetry said, shaking his head. "You're always sleepy in the morning, and we don't want you to fall out of the boat. Besides, we're going after northern pike, not walleye."

Dragonfly didn't like that very well, and Poetry really shouldn't have said it. Anyway, Dragonfly's face turned red, and he said, "All right then, smarties, I'll tell the whole gang right away!" He lifted his voice and shouted, "Hey, gang! Listen! Bill and—"

That was as far as Dragonfly got. We both grabbed him. I clapped my hand over his mouth, and Poetry said, "Of course, you can go, but for good sense's sake, *keep still!*" He whispered the last two words.

The gang all stopped and looked back and yelled for us to hurry up or we'd be late to Sunday school, so we hurried.

But the plan was still a secret, and we knew that tomorrow morning the little outboard motor would be going out across the lake—that is, if we could borrow Eagle Eye's rowboat so that we wouldn't be heard by any of the gang when we started out. The little motor weighed only fourteen pounds—we could carry it easily without getting tired.

Boy oh boy! Early tomorrow morning! It was great to think about! I'd rather have run an outboard motor than do anything—even better than I'd liked to ride my bicycle when it was new.

We hurried along behind the gang, hiking toward the strange new church. And pretty soon we were there.

11

At half past two that Sunday afternoon, we were all in the railroad car church. Big Jim and I sat together on one of the seats. Dragonfly and Tom Till were right across the aisle from us. A lot of Indians were there.

I won't take time to tell you all about it, but you ought to know that it was Little Jim who played for Circus's solo when he sang. It was great to look down the long aisle and up to the platform at the end and see that little brown-haired pal of mine sitting at the upside-down suitcase, pedaling away and playing it the way his very pretty mother does for our church back at Sugar Creek.

Circus stood behind the homemade wooden pulpit, lifted his head, and sang, shaking his head a little to emphasize his words, just as Santa had done in the morning. I don't know why I felt the way I did, but all of a sudden I couldn't swallow, and a second later I couldn't see very well either.

It was the same song I'd heard Circus sing before, and I got to thinking about how his father had been an alcoholic and had gotten bit by a black widow spider and then one night had been saved. And now Circus's whole family went to church, and maybe someday one of our Sugar Creek Gang was going to be very famous, and all the world would know about him.

I made up my mind that I was going to be as great as Circus would be, only I didn't exactly want to be *great*. I wanted to be—well, I wished I could be a Christian doctor who would save people's lives but that when people talked about me to each other, they wouldn't only say, "He's a great surgeon," but they'd say, "William Collins, M.D., is a famous Christian surgeon. He gives lots of money to help spread the Gospel."

As soon as Circus's solo was finished, Eagle Eye stood up and had us all stand. Then he shut his eyes and prayed a kind of long prayer in the Chippewa language. After that Barry gave a short sermon, and Santa and Mrs. Santa sang a duet, which was great, all about Jesus being "the Savior for me."

It was a sort of funny Sunday school because they kept everybody in one big class and different ones talked to us. After a while Santa had what is called a "testimony" meeting, and he asked everybody who wanted to, to stand up one at a time right where they were and tell, in just about ten words, where and when Jesus had saved them.

Santa said he was saved in Long Beach, California, in a tabernacle built on an old baseball field—on a spot that used to be first base.

Barry said, "I was saved in the hospital a year ago, when a Christian farmer from Sugar Creek came and talked to me."

And again I couldn't see straight. The crazy

old tears got all tangled with my eyes, and before I knew it I was on my feet and saying, "Yes, and that Christian farmer was my father! And—and he's the best dad in the world, and I was saved up in our haymow one day while I was praying and reading my New Testament."

Well, it didn't seem nearly as hard for me to stand up in that railroad car and say those words as I knew it would have been at home. The next thing I knew I was sitting down, and I guess I never was so happy in my life, which is the way a boy feels when he gets up like that in church.

One after another we stood. Circus and Big Jim and Poetry each knew *when* and *where*.

Then Little Jim stood up. He didn't say anything for a bit, then he said, with his Little Jim voice, "I don't know any special place where I was when I let Jesus come into my heart, but I know He's there!"

Quite a number of people who were not Indians had come out from town to attend that meeting, and when Little Jim said that, two or three men with big voices up in the front of the church, said, "Amen!"

I kept thinking about Dragonfly and wondering what he'd do or if he'd just keep still. But he stood right after Little Jim and said, "I got saved when I was sliding down out of a sycamore tree down along Sugar Creek, just like Zacchaeus did in the Bible."

That was all of us except Little Tom Till, the new member of our gang.

Pretty soon a lady stood and said something in Chippewa, which I couldn't understand but which had the word *Jesus* in it. Eagle Eye's mom and his father stood up too—and even Snow-in-the-Face. I was sitting right where I could look into his face, and I thought of all the interesting things I'd have to tell the folks when I got home.

All of a sudden, Tom Till was standing and gulping and trying to talk and couldn't, and then he did. This is what he said: "I—I don't know whether I'm s-saved or not, but I w-wish everybody in the world was, and especially my father and mother—" His voice choked off, and he sat down.

Eagle Eye was acting as interpreter, that is, he stood on the platform and said everything *we* said all over again in Chippewa, just as soon as we had said it, so that everybody there would understand. Well, when Tom Till said he didn't know whether he was saved or not but that he wished everybody in the world was, Eagle Eye said that was a good sign that maybe Little Tom Till *was*.

You know, there are a lot of people in the world who have opened their heart's door and invited Jesus to come in, and He has actually saved them, but they don't know the Bible well enough to *know* that having Jesus in the heart is the same as being saved.

Santa, who preached a short sermon right after that, explained that to us, stopping after nearly every sentence for Eagle Eye to interpret for him.

It was a good sermon, not very long but the kind that made a boy feel as if he wanted to be a fisherman like Peter and the other disciples in the Bible, who were always going fishing and having a lot of fun but who became what is called "soul winners," or fishers of *men*, instead of just fishers of fish.

While Santa was talking, I could almost see that beautiful big lake over there in Galilee with its pretty blue water dancing and sparkling in the sunlight. I could see the boats bobbing up and down on the water, with the big fish wriggling and bouncing around in them when they got pulled in.

And then I could picture Jesus standing over on the sandy shore where He had built a little fire that morning and was roasting fish for their breakfast. And I wondered if they knew how to cook an underground dinner, so they could let the fire go out and then fish for two hours and, when they were hungry, come back and eat.

I could see Peter, that big rough fisherman, who made me think of Big John Till, Tom's father, and maybe looked like him too. Only Peter became a fine Christian, and John Till was still an unsaved man.

Well, I could see Peter stop fishing all of a sudden, just as the Bible story says, and look over toward the shore to where blue smoke was rising from the little yellow-tongued fire, with flames leaping up like Circus's father's hounds do. And then Peter grabbed his fisherman's coat, tied it on, and went splashity-sizzle out across the shallow water toward shore.

Then the rest of the disciple-fishermen came to shore in a boat. When they got there, there weren't any big flames and not much smoke but just live coals with fish broiling on them, which goes to show that Jesus knew all about how to cook fish the best way—over an open fire.

It was a great story.

After the sermon was finished, Tom Till and I and a lot of Indian boys and girls were standing around the folding organ near the platform. Different people were talking to each other and looking at Little Jim play, which he kept on doing, his playing being called a *postlude*. Little Jim knew all about music and nearly all the musical terms—his mom, you know, was the best musician in all of Sugar Creek territory.

Pretty soon Santa walked over to Tom and stood in front of him. He reached out both of his big hands and put them on Tom's shoulders, looked at him with his big, soft brown eyes, and asked him something that I couldn't hear.

Little Tom Till dropped his head and nodded it, and a couple of tears squeezed themselves out of his eyes and fell down on Santa's shining black shoes, like a couple of sparkling diamonds falling. And I'll bet, if Jesus saw them fall, that those two little salty tears must have looked more important to Him than a whole truckload of jewelry.

Big Santa's big arm went around Little Tom,

and they walked toward a curtained-off place at the end of the railroad coach. I knew that in about a minute there'd be another member of the Sugar Creek Gang who was born again— which is an expression the Bible uses for becoming a Christian. And you have to be that or you aren't saved yet, no matter how good you think you are, Old Man Paddler says.

On the way home, as we were hiking back along the same way we'd come, all of us walking together, Circus surprised us by saying, "Guess what!"

We stopped walking, and Circus was looking up at a balsam tree as though he wished he didn't have on such good clothes, so that he could climb it.

"What's so important?" Dragonfly wanted to know.

And all of a sudden Circus forgot his clothes and went shinnying up that tree to the first limb, where he sat and looked down at us, grinning like a half-grown chimpanzee. Then he said, "I've been invited to go to Chicago to sing in Santa's church and over the radio."

I stared at him. Dragonfly picked up a stick and tossed it up at him. Big Jim's face was sober. Poetry started to quote a poem, picking up a handful of leaves and tossing them in the air and watching them blow away:

"As dry leaves before the hurricane fly,
    When they meet with an obstacle,
        mount to the sky,

So up to the housetop
   the coursers they flew,
With a sleigh full of toys,
   and St. Nicholas, too."

That verse is a part of the poem "The Night Before Christmas," and St. Nicholas is another name for Santa Claus.

Little Jim said, "Why didn't Santa invite all of us to come?"

"Why?" Circus called down to us. "Because it's at Thanksgiving time, and there wouldn't be enough turkey for all of us and Poetry too. The turkey would have to be as big as a roast lamb!"

"See if you can figure out this riddle," Poetry said, changing the subject:

"Two legs sat upon three legs
   With one leg in his lap;
In comes four legs
   And runs away with one leg;
Up jumps two legs,
   Catches up three legs,
Throws it after four legs,
   And makes him bring back one leg."

As soon as Poetry had finished, he said, "Give up?"

We finally gave up, and he explained it. "Man with two legs sits on three-legged stool with leg of lamb on his lap. Dog with four legs comes in, runs away with leg of lamb. Man with two legs jumps up, throws three-legged stool at dog and makes him bring back the leg of lamb! Now, hurry up, everybody, and let's get back to camp to supper."

Which we did.

But it was true. Circus was invited to go to Chicago, with all expenses paid, to sing in Santa's big church and also over the radio. Not only that, but he could ride to that big noisy city any way he wanted to, either on the train or on a bus, or he could go by airplane!

Imagine that! By *airplane!* You can guess that I felt like Little Jim did. "Why didn't Santa invite us all to come?"

"Maybe he will," Circus said, just as we came within sight of the camp.

And maybe he will. Who knows? If he does, I'll write about it for you.

And if he does, the Sugar Creek Gang will spend Thanksgiving vacation in one of the largest cities in the world. We'll see the zoo and the museum and store buildings that are as big as mountains. That would make a good title for a new story, wouldn't it? *The Chicago Adventure.*

Pretty soon it would be night and time to go to bed. And early in the morning, Poetry and Dragonfly and I would be out on the lake fishing for a twenty-pound northern pike. Boy, oh boy!

Barry sent Tom Till and me to gather wood for the campfire. Tom was very quiet while we picked up different-sized sticks, and I knew he was remembering what had happened to him in the railroad car church.

All of a sudden he said, "My big brother Bob's been workin' for your dad this week, hoein' potatoes."

"I know it," I said, and then that little red-haired guy said, "Do you suppose your mom'll give him an extra-large piece of blackberry pie?"

"Sure she will," I said, thinking about my mom's extra-kind face.

And then Tom Till said something that sounded just like something Little Jim would have thought of saying. He said, "I'll bet if your mom gives him an extra-big piece of blackberry pie—and is especially nice to him—maybe he'll think Jesus is all right too, and it'll be easier to get him to go to church."

When he said that, I sort of felt that he had said one of the most important things in the world.

Well, Tom and I came grunting back into camp with our big armloads of wood. Then he asked to borrow my binoculars, so he could look out across the lake to an island in the middle, where the sun was shining on the tops of the trees as though somebody had taken a paintbrush and splotched a lot of yellowish-red paint on them.

"Sure," I said, "here they are," handing my binoculars to him. "Keep them as long as you like," which he did, not giving them back until the next day, which was the day of all the excitement in camp, the day of the big fishing trip.

12

That night around the campfire, just before going to bed, Barry gave us five Bible verses to memorize. I wrote them down in a little notebook, where I had a lot of other important things a Christian boy ought to know. One of the verses ended like this: "Follow Me, and I will make you fishers of men."

Even though I was remembering the sermon Santa had preached in the afternoon, and even though I was actually listening to Barry's talk, I caught Poetry's eye across the fire, and he winked at me, meaning, *Tomorrow morning early.*

And that reminds me—I forgot to tell you that right after the meeting in the railroad coach, Poetry and Dragonfly and I had asked Eagle Eye if we could borrow his rowboat tomorrow morning early, and he said we could and had handed us the key so we could unlock it.

So when Poetry winked at me, my hand slid into one of my pockets and brought out the key, which I held half hidden, yet so Poetry could see it. Dragonfly saw it too, but I looked at him with my eyebrows down so he wouldn't look happy and make the rest of the gang wonder what mischief was afoot.

We even arranged it so that the three of us could sleep in the same tent that night. Whichever one of us should awaken first in the morning was supposed to waken the rest of us.

I crawled into my sleeping bag, zipped up the zipper, pulled the nice warm blankets close around my chin, because the nights were always cold up there, and pretty soon I was a goner, which means I was asleep. I didn't know anything —although, of course, when a boy is asleep and doesn't know anything, he doesn't know it.

Right away, it seemed, I was awake again. Something feeling like a kitten's feet was jumping up and down on my stomach. I was terribly sleepy and didn't want to wake all the way up, but I supposed it was Poetry or Dragonfly, so I made myself open my eyes.

It wasn't even daylight yet inside the tent, although I could see out through a little crack where the tent flap was open toward the east. I could hear two people breathing, one on each side of me, so I knew Poetry and Dragonfly were still asleep. Yet *something* was bouncing around on my stomach, something that had little feet and was using all of them.

You can guess I woke up in a hurry. I sneaked my hand under my pillow for my flashlight, turned it on, and stared at what I saw.

It was a wild animal! An actual wild animal. A wild cat!

No, not a *wildcat*, but a wild polecat, which is a skunk! I could smell him; and anybody who knows what a skunk smells like doesn't like it.

That little black-and-white skunk stopped bouncing on my stomach when I flashed the light on him and just stared at the light, with his two green eyes looking like two tiny flashlights shining right in my face.

Before I knew it, I'd hissed, *"Scat!"*

That woke Poetry, and he jumped as if somebody had punched him in the ribs. He threw back his blankets and sat straight up, grabbing his nose quick with one hand.

Well, that scared the skunk, and he whirled around like a flash with his big, bushy black-and-white tail straight up in the air, which meant he was angry, or scared, or excited and was going to spray his ridiculous perfume all over the tent. I'd seen skunks do that back along Sugar Creek when one of Circus's dad's dogs was about to catch it.

"Duck!" I whispered fiercely to Poetry, which he did, and which I did even quicker.

Mr. Skunk, however, must have had good home training or else he wasn't excited enough, for he ran like a kitten straight for the tent flap and went out, leaving enough of his unnecessary perfume behind him to make us want to get out too.

Dragonfly, as you already know, was always sleepy in the morning, but all of a sudden he woke up, grabbed his nose, and said, "What on earth!"

Poetry shushed him, saying in a hoarse whisper, "We've just had company."

"Wh-what time is it?" Dragonfly asked.

I looked at my luminous-dialed watch, and it was 4:30. I stuck my head out through the tent flap and looked toward the northeast, where the sun was supposed to rise. The sky was already a sort of pearlish pink. It was time to get up to go to catch that twenty-pound northern pike.

We dressed, whispering. Then we crept out quietly so as not to awaken the gang in the other tent and in the trailer, picked up the outboard motor and our fishing tackle, and hurried up the lakeshore toward Eagle Eye's rowboat.

At the edge of the woods we stopped to take stock: fishing tackle; live minnows for bait, which we'd kept in the live box at the end of the dock and now had in a minnow pail; the little fourteen-pound motor, which Dragonfly was carrying by the rubber grip on its steering handle; and a can of gasoline, because the motor ran out of gas about every hour. Yes, we had everything we needed. Our life preservers were already tied on good and tight.

Pretty soon we were there. I climbed into the boat first, taking the motor with me. I went back to the stern and sat down and began to attach it. While I was tightening the thumb screw button, Poetry unlocked the boat. Dragonfly arranged the tackle box and the minnows so we could each reach for an extra minnow without having to stretch too far.

In a jiffy we were ready. We shoved off and floated out until we were out far enough for the motor to run without its propeller getting tangled up with the sandy bottom.

I felt proud to think I could start the motor all by myself. I was glad there wasn't anybody older there to tell me how to do it, when I already *knew* how. When a boy knows how to do something, he almost gets mad inside when somebody older than he is starts to explain things and to tell him just exactly how to do it —although you can't expect all the parents in the world to know that.

First, I opened the air vent screw and the gasoline shutoff valve, then coiled the starter rope around the starting disc, moved the mixture lever over to number four on the dial, and did what I was supposed to do to the carburetor float pin.

There was already plenty of gasoline in the tank, so I was ready. Quick as a flash I pulled the starter rope, and just as quick the motor started, and we were off, puttity-sizzle out onto the lake. I made a few adjustments, which I'd learned how to make, and throttled the motor down to what is called trolling speed, which is very slow, with the motor barely running and the boat barely creeping over the water. *Maybe Old Northern is on this side of the neck today,* I thought. The water was very quiet on this side.

I sat there with my left hand on the rubber grip on the steering handle, feeling important, feeling happy, and feeling as if something was going to happen.

Poetry had his line in the water, letting it

trail along about fifty feet behind the boat and with a sinker heavy enough to keep the bait just as close to the bottom of the lake as possible without catching the weeds that grew down there. I didn't even put my line in the water, because I wanted to run the boat.

Dragonfly sat in the prow and kept his line out too.

All of us felt fine. The weather was just a little chilly, as it is in the early morning up there. I steered along the shoreline, following the long neck of land down toward its point, staying about twenty or thirty feet out from the bulrushes growing near the shore.

The water was very quiet, and every now and then we could see a splash at the edge of the weeds where a bass was probably getting his breakfast. In the east, the big, round sun stuck its face out from under the earth, where it had been buried all night, wiggled its head through a couple of reddish-pink clouds, and started off on its day's work.

"Look!" Dragonfly said all of a sudden.

Poetry and I looked just in time to see a great blue heron, with wings as long as a boy, start flying from the shore out across the lake.

I tell you, I felt good. I also felt sorry for all the people in the world who ought to take a vacation and couldn't afford it, and I thought that all those people in the world who *could* afford a rest like the one we were having, and *didn't* take it, were just plumb crazy.

Santa says that even Jesus told His disciples

to "come away . . . and rest a while," and He Himself would go out into the mountains or somewhere where He could be alone with the heavenly Father and get His soul rested.

I made up my mind that when I grew up I'd take my boys—or let them go alone—to some camp where there was real Bible training. And I'd teach them to love the great big out-of-doors, which God made for us to enjoy.

I didn't have time to think long though—not much longer than it took that big, blue, awkward bird to gallop across the corner of the sky to another shore. For suddenly Dragonfly got what is called a strike, which means that a fish somewhere down in the lake was hungry and had made a headfirst dive straight toward his hook and got caught.

Right away Dragonfly's eyes were wider open than ever, and he was pulling in a fish.

It wasn't much of a fish, though. Just about fifteen inches long, a walleyed pike. He put it on the stringer without my even stopping the motor, and we put-putted along with Poetry looking kind of sober.

"What do you bet I get my big northern?" he asked.

"You won't," I said.

And just then his pole went down against the side of the boat with a *whack*, his reel started to sing fiercely, and Poetry's eyes looked the way Dragonfly's had. Something had grabbed his line. "I—I've g-got him!" he stammered, and it looked as if he had.

Away back behind the boat there was a fierce boiling of the water, and up through the surface lunged a big snout with a body fastened to it as long as Poetry's leg—almost. It actually looked as big as Little Jim.

The fight was on. All week, Poetry had not only been watching Barry and others catch big fish, but he had been reading up on what to do in case he got one on *his* line. Any fisherman knows that if you try to pull a big fish straight into the boat when you have just a little pole and the line tests only about twenty-five pounds, the fish'll break your line as if it was a spider-web and maybe break your pole too. You have to let the fish get tired out first.

So every time that big, fierce fish started to run down toward the bottom of the lake, or in some other direction, Poetry let his reel run with it. Then, just the very second he got a chance, he'd start winding up the line again.

"Let him go! Let him go!" Dragonfly yelled, as excited as Poetry was.

Zing! Out went Poetry's line with the reel spinning like an automobile wheel in a race.

I shoved the steering handle over to the left so the boat would go around in a circle, just the way I'd seen Barry do it. But all of a sudden Old Northern decided he didn't like the water along the shore, and he started out into deeper water. Poetry's line was unwinding faster all the time, which meant that as soon as it had all unwound, the fish would snap the line and be gone.

Without taking time to think, I opened the

throttle, and our boat leaped into the race, with Poetry acting like an expert fisherman. He wound up his reel as fast as he could, while sweat ran down his face and his breath acted as if he was in a fierce footrace.

Then, away ahead of us, the water broke open, and up shot Old Northern, his ugly snout about as long as a big dog's head. He stayed out of the water only as long as it took him to get back in again, but we got to see all of him. While he was up in the air he shook his vicious old head savagely like a dog shaking a rat, trying to shake the hook out of his mouth, but he couldn't. Then he disappeared, and Poetry's line went tight.

"He's gone to the bottom!" Poetry puffed.

I steered in the direction of the fish, and it looked as if Poetry was right. The monster had dived straight to the bottom of the lake and maybe had buried itself in the weeds.

Poetry tugged on the line, but it was just like pulling on a line when the hook is fastened to a log.

"M-maybe he th-threw the hook out!" Dragonfly said, his teeth chattering. He wasn't cold, though—only excited and scared.

Poetry grunted in disgust and kept on winding in his line while I steered in a circle, getting closer and closer to the place where the line must have been fastened to the bottom of the lake.

I was beginning to notice now that the waves were a lot higher than they had been. In fact, they were rocking our boat too much for comfort. I looked up and saw we were just even with the end of the point of land where the waves were blowing past. And before we could do anything about it, we were out in them.

It had been quiet on our side of the point, because that side had been protected from the wind, but out here the wind came across in a big sweep, and the waves were rolling twice as high as our boat.

But there we were! I opened the throttle full force for a minute, but that little motor couldn't any more battle against those waves than a baby could battle a windstorm. Yes, there we were! A big northern pike on Poetry's line, and a fierce wind that we couldn't buck!

Then like a sudden thunderclap scaring a boy, Old Northern came to life down there in the lake bottom and started running wild again, just as the boat began to toss around in almost every direction at once.

"Can't you *guide* the thing?" Poetry yelled at me. "Steer over there toward the sheltered place behind the point!"

"Steer nothing!" I yelled. "This baby can't make it! It's too little!"

I caught a glimpse of Dragonfly in the prow, holding onto both sides with his knuckles white.

But Poetry didn't seem to have any sense for anything but the northern. He didn't know we were getting into rough water, or, if he did, he was just thinking about how hard it was to catch the fish.

Waves tossed us around as though our boat was a matchstick and the motor wasn't any more than an electric fan.

Still, in a little while Poetry had Old Northern up close to the boat, and that big fellow with his savage-looking eyes and teeth was acting tired. At the same time, I discovered how to keep the boat headed *against* the waves and not let it run in what is called the "trough."

We were actually making headway back toward the point of land and quiet water when Poetry leaned over too far and overbalanced the boat. It shipped water—a whole half boatful in one big gulp, as though it was thirsty and wanted to take in the whole lake.

Dragonfly screamed, and so did I. Poetry lunged back to the other side of the boat, just as Dragonfly and I did the same thing.

The boat capsized, and all of us were out in the water.

13

In the water! With a hard wind blowing and beginning to blow harder, the way it often does in the morning just after sunrise! And as the waves got higher, the farther out we drifted!

Barry had taught us all what to do in case a boat ever tipped over or filled up with water and we didn't happen to have on our life preservers.

"Stay with the boat!" he had ordered in a loud voice, driving it into our heads like a carpenter hitting a nail hard to drive it into a piece of wood. "Stay with the boat! *Don't* try to swim to shore with your clothes on! Keep your body all the way under except for your head and get to the boat and hold on! Even if it is filled with water, it won't sink unless you try to get in. Stay down low, and hold onto the boat, and let the wind blow you to some shore!"

Then Barry had told us to do the same thing if we were in a canoe and it turned over. "People who stay with the canoe and hold onto it never drown!" Barry said. "It's only those people who leave it and try to swim to shore who drown. Remember that! *Canoes never sink!* They do get overbalanced easily unless you keep your weight low in them, but they *never sink!*"

Well, we knew all those rules, but already

we were a long way from the boat, which was right side up again but was, of course, full of water. Besides, we had on our life preservers.

I looked over to my right, and there was Dragonfly struggling around, gulping and gasping, but his head was above the water. I knew he couldn't drown unless he stuck his head under the water himself, because his life preserver was holding him up. He was riding up and down, up and down with the high waves, which had whitecaps on them and looked like a lot of live, mad snowdrifts.

Just that minute I had to think about myself, because a big wave picked me up and threw me over into the center of a low place, so that there were high waves on each side of me. About all I could see was the sky above and high water on each side.

I don't know how I happened to think of it then, but I did. I thought of the Bible story that tells about God's people hurrying down to the Red Sea over in Egypt. The angry Egyptians were behind them with war chariots and spears, ready to kill them. Then Moses lifted up the rod he had in his hand and stretched it out over the sea, and the water stood straight up on each side, so the people could walk right across the sea as if they were walking through a long hall.

My dad says that God did that for a special purpose and that He does the same thing for us today, only in a different way. When people have to wade through a lot of trouble, He makes the trouble stand up on each side so they can go through safely and their souls will come out all right on the other side.

Old Man Paddler, I thought, had gone through a lot of trouble like that, and he hadn't ever drowned yet.

Well, I'd had rides on what is called the Tilt-a-Whirl at a county fair, and they had been lots of fun. I knew that if I could quit feeling scared, I'd have one of the longest, happiest, Tilt-a-Whirl rides a boy could ever have, because, remember, we couldn't drown as long as our heads were above water, which they were all the time.

I heard Poetry holler just then. Looking behind me, I saw that he still had hold of that fishing pole, and the fish was still on the other end of the line.

The only thing was, if Old Northern would decide he wanted to take a trip down to the bottom of the lake, and if the bottom happened to be farther down than the length of Poetry's line, Poetry'd either have to let go, or else be pulled under, or else his line would break.

It's a crazy feeling, being about a mile out in a lake, in the water from your shoulders down and riding the waves, especially when the water feels cold. I was glad there weren't any sharks there to eat us up.

Just then I heard a splash behind me, and it was Dragonfly swimming toward me with a grin on his face. "It's what I kind of hoped would happen," he said, his teeth chattering again, "but I wish I wasn't so s-scared."

He reached out to grab hold of me, but I yelled for him not to, because it would be safer for each one of us to be by himself.

"I want something to hold onto!" he yelled back.

We'd have worked our way over to the boat, but it was drifting faster than we were, so there was nothing for us to do but what we were doing, which was nothing—except that Poetry still held onto his fishing pole.

"I've still got him!" he puffed and grinned at me as though he was having the time of his life. "What are you looking so scared ab—" Poetry stopped as a big wave tossed him around and splashed up into his face. But he was grinning again in a minute. "No use to be scared," he said. "See the island over there! We'll be there in about fifteen minutes, and then I'll land my fish."

Just the same, I was glad we weren't adrift in any ocean or on a big lake that didn't *have* an island.

When a boy is badly scared, he can't get over it right away either. I kept on feeling funny around my heart and thinking a lot of tangled-up thoughts, such as it was a good thing Little Jim and I had had our strange ride on the hog house in Sugar Creek that spring, or our parents wouldn't have made us wear life preservers when we went out in the boat up here. I also thought that even if a lake was awfully deep, it wouldn't take a drowning boy long to get to the bottom.

We kept on drifting, calling out different things to each other, and beginning to feel almost cheerful when we saw ourselves getting nearer and nearer the island.

Poetry actually called out to me once, "Say, Bill! What direction are we floating?"

That made me think that, on a map that was hanging on a wall, straight south was *straight down!!* So I yelled back at him, just as a big wave came between us and we couldn't see each other, "If we hadn't put on our life preservers, we'd have all floated straight *south.* "

Even though we still didn't *feel* safe, I knew we were. Yet my feelings and what I knew kept arguing with each other, with my feelings getting the best of the argument most of the time. For a minute I thought of what Little Jim, the best Christian in our gang and maybe in the whole world, would say if he was with us. I thought maybe he'd say something like this, "That goes to show that if a boy has Jesus for his Savior, he is *saved*, whether he feels it all the time or not."

In another five or ten minutes, though, we'd be to the island, and there maybe we could start a fire with a bow and a stick and some string, as Barry'd been teaching us how to do, and we could send up smoke signals the way Scouts do, and somebody would see them and come to our rescue. It'd be fun being marooned on an island for a while.

"Heyl Look!" Dragonfly called to us. "The wind's going to blow us *past* the island!"

We looked, and Dragonfly was right. We *were* going to miss the island, unless—unless we could swim a little against those waves and keep from drifting by. If we drifted past the island, we'd have to drift for a lot of miles before we'd ever get to land, because the shore on the other side of it was a long way off.

Just then Poetry yelled, "Now this crazy old northern's got himself buried on the bottom of the lake and won't budge." He was holding his pole up in the air, and the reel was spinning around and around as the waves washed him toward me.

"Jerk him!" I called back. "Make him mad! Then maybe he'll—"

Poetry jerked. A minute later he was winding in his line again, which meant the fish was following along behind us somewhere.

And just that minute I heard a roaring. It sounded like an airplane. I looked up but didn't see anything. I did see that we were going to miss the island, so I hollered to Poetry to let the fish go and to start to swim, or we'd have to stay in the water maybe all the rest of the morning.

But it was too late. Dragonfly was already starting past the island, and I would be in a minute, and so would Poetry.

"Look!" Dragonfly cried again. "Somebody's coming in a boat!"

Again he was right. Straight toward us from across the lake came a big white boat that looked like Santa's. A high-powered motor was carrying that boat roarity-sizzle toward the island and us!

"Hurrah!" I yelled. "We're saved!"

And we were! It *was* Santa's boat. In the prow was Little Tom Till, holding on tight and with his life preserver on, and back in the stern were Barry and Big Jim.

It didn't take us long to get rescued after that. Dragonfly and I were in the boat in a jiffy.

Poetry was still holding onto his fishing pole. Just as quick as he was in, he started working on Old Northern, and within about three minutes, with a big gaff hook that Barry had in the boat, we had landed him.

Talk about a fish! We never did quit talking about it, Poetry especially.

It was a wet but happy boatful of people that went back across those high waves, roarity-sizzle, toward camp. And it was a tired and hungry three of us who, after we'd changed clothes, sat down with Barry at the dinette end of the trailer and ate pancakes and bacon and grapefruit for breakfast.

"How'd you know where to find us?" I asked, sort of chopping off the last two words when I bit off a nice juicy bite of pancake.

"Easy," Barry said. "Tom was out looking at the lake with your binoculars, and he saw you."

You can guess we were glad we'd invited Little Tom Till to go along with us on our camping trip!

Maybe I ought to tell you—before we came back from the island, we pulled Eagle Eye's boat up onto the shore away from the waves and took the little motor off and brought it back with us. As soon as the lake got quiet again, we'd go back to the island and get it.

The motor would have to have something done to it, of course, because it was all water soaked. I was just glad it had stayed fastened onto the boat, or it would have been lying down on the bottom of the lake somewhere, as Barry says hundreds of motors are all over America because somebody has been careless or has had an accident he couldn't help.

Well, I looked across the table at Dragonfly and Poetry and then down the length of the trailer at Big Jim and Circus and Little Jim and Tom, sitting there on the davenport, watching us eat and listening to us talk. I was very glad to be alive. Everything was quiet for a minute, and I could hear the drip-drip of water as the ice slowly melted in the icebox.

Just then Little Jim turned around to where the radio was sitting on the shelf behind him and turned it on. "It's time for the 'Children's Gospel Hour,'" he said. And in a minute we heard the voices of a lot of boys and girls singing a chorus we'd learned only a few nights before at our campfire:

"Broadcast the gospel everywhere,
    Tell it to sinners far and near;
Christ, God's Son upon Calvary's tree,
    Paid the ransom for you and for me;
Broadcast the gospel everywhere."

Between songs, I asked Circus, "Will you dedicate a song to us when you get to Chicago next Thanksgiving?"

"Sure," Circus said, grinning. "I'll even dedicate a piece of turkey to you when I eat it," which made Poetry frown and made me wish harder than ever that Santa would invite the whole gang to go along with Circus. I'd never had an airplane ride. And I'd never been in Chicago. Or in a broadcasting studio.

Looking back over this story, I see it's as long as it ought to be. So I'll have to skip all the things that happened the second week of our camping trip. It was a great week, though, and we had the time of our lives.